Brian Miller

&

the Twins of Triton

J. Michael Brower

Brian Miller

&

the Twins of Triton

~Book One~

A Trilogy by J. Michael Brower

Peacock Press of Pasadena

Pasadena, Maryland

Acknowledgement:

For Joe

CONTENTS

CHAPTER ONE
Worlds of Indifference

I'm Katrina.

Katrina Ivanovna Chakiaya.

Geezum crow, what a mouth full!

So my friend Brian Miller thinks. He watches over my shoulder as I write a brief intro. You see, I wasn't there for all of it. And some only my father knows.

I'm from Russia. But Brian thinks it best if we begin at our high school — the school we were to share.

I

It was on the secretary's semi-nasty schedule: "B. Miller, 1300".

This was going to suck — big time. Principal Robert Brodsky threw himself into his creaky swivel chair. I prepared for some real smack-action. It was impossible to say which was more ancient — the principal, the cryptic chair or our surreal school. People were talking about my rescuing the Pellitier kid. I knew I'd end up in front of geezer Brodsky. Bellows Free Academy, the high school for little Saint

Albans, Vermont, had been built in the early 1930s, a Great Depression project. It was little and cramped. "I've a complaint that you jumped Justin, Dirk and Derek and took some money. Brian, the only reason I'm trying to handle this internally is because it'd just kill your mother to have you in trouble. Damn it, Brian!" The principal slammed his hand on the desk, made me jump. He got up.

If he hears about the heroin, too, I'm done.

"Is everything alright, Mr. Brodsky?"

It was that nose-picking secretary, Ms. Ashline. Her problem was so bad, I thought her head would cave in.

"Yes, Ms. Ashline. Brian here's have trouble controlling his temper."

"Umph," she snorted. Probably had her finger jammed to the second knuckle. She shut the door.

"Look, Brian—" Mr. Brodsky began, but I jumped in.

"—Mr. Brodsky, lemme tell you how it was. Justin's bunch were jackin' up Allen and—"

"—I'll tell you what," Brodsky double-interrupted, whacking at the air as if my words were gnats. "Winter break is over and I wanted you to return with a clean slate."

Man, how do I get out of this one?

I tried to stay cool, but the room was very hot. It was only 20 degrees outside, but the many radiators around each of the six huge windows in the room were on maximum overdrive. They hissed—I felt like hissing back. The walls were red (well, 'maroon' then!) making it even hotter. I wiped off beads of forehead sweat. It's often gray with clouds in Vermont. The windows are build extra large to capture the sun.

2

"Mr. Miller," Mr. Brodsky wasn't smiling.

"Here's the kid who opened his last year in middle school by pushing Sandra Suntag out of the way of a truck. Just in time, as I hear it. Her wheelchair was stuck in our broken sidewalks. No one has money for the most important things. Like taking care of handicapped folks? Well, we've still got a long way to go, as a species, Brian. We just don't have our priorities straight, kid. I'd hate to have to justify our actions to anybody in real authority. Great graduation present for this high school."

I looked up.

"Saving the Suntag kid was a good on you. But it cost us. It cost money to fix those sidewalks after her parents sued the middle school. Maybe unintended consequences should be cautionary tales. Your helping people out seems to be a double-edged sword, Mr. Miller—I see a real pattern here. You help but you makes things worse too, 'notice? Now Allen and the Esteridge girl will have to watch their backs, thanks to you...what next?"

"You told Justin to leave them alone, right? It's my fault—no one else's."

"I'll ask the questions."

So I shut my mouth.

"Sure. Also told the parents involved," went on Brodsky. "Does that make you feel like everything will be okay for them in these halls? What about after school?"

I didn't know what to say. I wanted out of that office. My drug habit, even though it was brand new, had a hold of me. It was...overpowering. It was only two weeks—and I was sick.

3

"Listen up, Miller. This is real-time sunshine," Mr. Brodsky's coffee breath was overpowering and nasty. "There are consequences, in real life, for doing the right thing. You're a smart kid. You'll figure it out — or I'll end up throwing you out." He returned to his seat. It creaked in agony, like a tree with its roots cut.

It was all I could do to wait for dismissal.

And that hit…got to have it, can't wait for school to get out!

"Brian Miller; the kid how recently grabbed the class fire extinguisher to put out the flames about to swallow up ol' Mr. Abair, our favorite chemistry teacher. You saved him from serious injury when his old tweed coat caught fire during a Bunson Burner experiment before winter break. I never saw him wear anything else in this school but that old blazer. Lucky for you the hospital's up the street. But you did send him to the hospital to get his eyes flushed of fire retardant, too?"

I winced like a pointy paper airplane had crashed into my cheek.

"It wasn't like I had a gun saving Allen."

"Don't get sassy with me. I'm not your buddy."

"Sorry, sir."

"You seem to have a lot of ready answers, Brian. You may discover situations too complex for pat responses. Real life doesn't cut the kind of breaks you're getting here. In human society, it's like you're in a framework. You try to go beyond it, you get smacked. Pushback is hard. You seem a little too swift for a freshman," Mr. Brodsky sounded jealous. He was right, as I found out.

"Not swift enough to keep out of your office," I managed.

"Touché."

"Can I go?"

"Brian, stay out of trouble. Stop trying to save the world, let it find its own way, don't you think?"

"Uh, hmm-mm, sure, I guess, Mr. Brodsky. Clean slate?"

"Not quite. And the world, Brian? *It can take care of itself!*" Principal Brodsky sat back in his chair to hear my answer.

I headed for the door. I couldn't keep from a reply.

"What kind of difference can one kid make, anyhow."

"You're asking me or telling me, Mr. Miller?" Then the phone rang on his desk. The principal jerked up the black receiver. And I left without answering his question. A good thing, because I was out of answers; my day had crumbled, now...it was all...all uncertainty. I left with the door open.

II

Escaped again — you the man! Now for a rush! One last hit before we see that dude...that dude in the shadows, downtown...the flatlander in the doorway...who said I should go see him? Now who was that?

I was relieved to be back in the lively halls, with my morbid thoughts. Other teens and occasional instructors, bound for classes, everyone talking. My hands shook, but no one noticed. The old coot was right. I couldn't guess all the consequences of my 'good deeds'.

About ten dudes in school were seriously out to get me. Some were just jealous. Some of the girls found me...*pretty*. I always wore plain gray T-shirts and old blue jeans. My hair was, and still is, too long. My oval glasses gave me a radical look...but I don't need those anymore.

"Hiiii, Brrriiiaaaannn," some of the girls would say.

"Yo, Bri! Best watch your back, man!"

"Brian, how's it going! 'Got last night's homework for me, dude?" from the needy. I usually helped all who asked.

"Miller! We're lookin' for you, boy, fo' shizzle! After school, you and me,'" once in a while.

Occasionally I'd exchange insults with someone. It's just part of high school life. We weren't allowed to swear. That was disallowed, there was a whole list of words we couldn't use. First offense, one hour detention; second, two hours; third, one day suspension. Mr. Brodsky's crazy rules, but parents approved.

"Hey, Bri, ya frickin' 'tard," some loser would say carefully, looking for teachers, as we passed in the hall. We slowed like two old men-o'-wars to exchange verbal cannon fire.

"Up yours, simp'!"

"Get bent, knob!"

"Crap licker!"

"Plumber's crack!"

"'You feeb'!"

"You sinkin' burp!"

"You gob."

"Turd face."

"Mental crip'."

"Short-buser"

"Your mother's a bigger one."

"I'll slap the taste out your mouth, Miller!"

When you got into the family tree, you had to be careful. Save that for out-of-fist-range. You never know, some people just can't take an insult. They go nuts on you.

In my classmates I saw admiration, jealousy, some hate, and some pity over my unwanted popularity. It wasn't a big school. It wasn't a big town. It was a small place. We had small lives.

I'd hit the bathroom and drop my bag inside the stall. I never used the urinals because you can get pushed in from the back. I always stood sideways over the bowl (dah!), just in case someone kicked in the door. The locks weren't any good. Oh, and of course number two was positively out.

My birthday is in January. I hoped that my "bad luck" year would become a better 14th year. But the drugs would ruin everything. Somehow I managed to get through the day without visiting the heroin in my locker. I wouldn't make it the next day. Not short of a miracle, anyhow.

CHAPTER TWO
Worlds So Out of Touch

"Class we have two announcements," said Ms. Claire Blodgett.

I was afraid I, Katrina, was on the list. She was speaking in front of the 9th grade Social Studies class. I felt awkward and from another country — which I was. But that's how you feel your first day in a new school; in a new town; on another continent. You have to endure. I stared at my desk like there was something important on it somewhere.

Outside the huge windows, I could see my new country-state-city's version of winter showing itself off. It beat on the windows with gusts of wind. But I knew my winter could send this one home crying. With a bloody nose; it's tail between its legs; head down; humiliated. My winter took no prisoners. It had beaten the ching chong out of Napoleon and Hitler. So it could kick Vermont's butt, too. Stupid winter!

The iron radiators were hissing at me — I, too, wanted to hiss back. I bit my lip. The name on the card nearly knocked the poor woman unconscious.

"First I'd like to introduce a new student. All the way from Russia! Over the summer, she'll be joining her father, a diplomat in Montreal. And she's staying with her uncle, an immigration officer with roots in Russia! We can learn so much about her home country from her! Things have changed a lot there in the last decade," she paused a moment.

Putting a hand to her chin, she almost burnt a hole in the index card with her nearly crossed eyes. "So let me introduce…er…Kath — Kathy — Karina (oh, the hurricane, isn't it?) — I — Ivan — Ivan — *Ivanonva* Cheek — Chu — Chakiaya! Geezum crow, there's a mouth full! May we just call you Kathy?"

She pronounced the "Ivan" part like non-Russians do, with an "I" not an "E," but that was the best part of the butchering. Ms. Blodgett smiled sweetly, displaying her mouthful of horrid, randomly arranged, brownish teeth. My father, an officer and a scientist in Russia, had been transferred to Montreal on a diplomatic mission. He thought my attendance at Brian's "good working class school" what do me good. Yuck. Yuck and pooh!

And apparently Vermont has no dentists. Score for socialized medicine.

Though everyone was staring at me, one had a sympathetic look. Since I needed the comfort, I looked up. It was Brian Miller. He held a yellow-covered book, George Orwell's <u>Homage to Catalonia</u>. He told me about it later, extra credit for English. But I turned away.

"Ma'am, I'd prefer Katrina," I said in my British English. Great, know the language but still suffer for the accent. Whatever's fair.

"Isn't she a snot," I heard one kid whisper.

"Maybe we'll get a chance to have some fun with that one." I was to learn the members of the Mack Gang.

One look told me Justin, Derek and Dirk were conservative when it came to thinking—no sense in wasting any effort on it. I thought of a few psychological games I could try on them. A second glance, and I knew it would be reading bedtime stories to my brother Ivan's goldfish. Impact—minimal.

"All right," said Ms. Blodgett. "Um, yes...ah, the other announcement is that we're having two student teachers for the rest of the year. We've never had student teachers in our school before. We should all appreciate our little school being given this kind of attention by the University of Vermont. I'll soon introduce Mr. Joe Triassic and Ms. Leah Starblue." The names brought a raised gray eyebrow from Ms. Blodgett. She looked closely at the names on her note card. All these odd Flatlander names—*Geezumhood crow*!

For me, I was glad the attention would turn to others.

"Well," she continued and tediously went on, "Please make our newcomers feel welcome. The teacher aids—er, student teachers—will be instructing several different subjects, substituting for your regular teachers...as appropriate." Ms. Blodgett tightened her invisible lips and pushed her glasses up the bridge of her lengthy nose.

"Let's take out our schedules, since this is your homeroom for our new year," Ms. Blodgett said. As soon as she'd turned her back, Dirk, Justin and Derek swiveled around in their chairs, gawking at me. They were distracted by Brian's cold stare. I could see it was everything the three could do to keep from

leaping on him instantly. Brian looked like a fit
enough kid, but nothing like our boys from the state
gymnastics school. The Mack gang looked like too
much for him. Also, I noticed his right hand was
shaking.

Ms. Starblue walked in and what a wild sight she
was, even for fashion-crippled Vermont! Her clothes
were from someone's (desecrated) attic corner. Easily
six feet tall and somewhat stooped over, the woman
regarded the class with a slightly worried look, as
though she had never seen so many kids in one place
together. It was the look of someone unsure of
whether they should take the last cookie on the plate.
Then it's gone. She had the look of a parent trying to
park the car, and losing their nerve. The spot goes to
another driver. It's a kind of hesitancy that a kid can't
help but love to see. She could have been in her 40s
or 60s, it was hard to tell. She was conservatively
dressed, but her clothes seemed better suited for
another era — the blouse was a plaid, as in rhyming
with 'bad', Brian says, (and not the good kind of bad,
either, just YUCK!). Her hair was long, but pulled
back, severely tied with nothing more than a piece of
ribbon — odd looking, cheap ribbon. Impossible to
say exactly what color the single piece of material
was, it fluttered and seemed to change its shade as the
wearer moved, but slowly, subtly, like a flower
opening its petals or seaweed swaying in the ocean.
Wearing a plaid blouse, of course, she was nervous —
definitely cruel (and I know it!). She wore no glasses,
but looked like she should have, for her face seemed
wizened with study. Her eyes were light green with a
very pale blue line about the iris. The eyes flashed
about. I thought she was wearing those gaudy
contact lens that mess up eye color. Her gaze was not

friendly. The lips, thin, were not curved in anything like a smile. This student teacher wasn't looking to make nice with us.

The room hushed, not a whisper.

The woman was still looking around the room. Then she saw me. And at that moment, a slight smile did appear—but only for a second, and it was more of a smirk than anything else. She looked me up and down quickly and then actually tossed her head! I think she wanted to insult me. Now, I'm sure of it. Then she saw Brian and gave him a crooked, mean-girl little grin that lasted longer, and ended in a snear.

"Class, this is Ms. Leah Starblue," Ms. Blodgett said, driving her glasses up the two-hour nose. The name drew some giggles and a few mocking croaks. I looked at Brian who was glancing over at a kid I later learned was Allen Pellitier. Allen looked stressed out, but I saw him try to take some pleasure in the laughable student teacher.

"Ms. Starblue will be with us to the end of the year and hails from the University of Vermont's teaching degree program, one I went through myself," she smiled at her index card. It was handed her by Ms. Starblue upon entering the classroom. "Her specialties are math, science, social studies and physical education."

Brian and I exchanged another glance. The moment she finished the introduction, another person entered the room with a card in hand, on cue. He greeted Ms. Blodgett with a warm smile. He almost missed Ms. Blodgett's little fingers entirely in his large, outstretched hand.

"And this is Mr. Joe Triassic," once again, the nose of Ms. Blodgett's nose wriggled, her glasses slipped. I could tell that anything out of the ordinary somehow had an effect on her mondo, parking-lot four eyes.

Mr. Triassic was tall, but not just tall. He looked a refugee from professional basketball. Unlike Ms. Starblue, Mr. Triassic did at least attempt to smile at us. But like the first teacher, his clothing seemed about 30 years out of date, sporting a very old suit with highwaters. Giggles escaped and one kid just covered his face with laughter, and said something like "OhmaGauggggddd!"

"Mr. Triassic, you'll be teaching English and history, according to this."

"Correct, ma'am," said he with hands clasped behind his back, awkwardly shifting his prodigious, but apparently toned, weight. He had a crew cut and either blond or white hair, you couldn't tell.

"You're specialties in college?" asked Ms. Blodgett.

"Very recently my specialties, yes."

"You're a native Vermonter?"

"No, ma'am."

"So formal, I almost thought you were."

"Apologies," said he, igniting more student snickering. He looked like he couldn't get out of his own big way, like he could trip himself just standing there so awkwardly. We students all wondered the same thing — were these student teachers going to be difficult or just harmless clowns?

"Mr. Triassic has a lot to learn, Ms. Blodgett," chimed in Ms. Starblue, apologetically.

"May I ask if you, perhaps, are a native Vermonter?" responded Ms. Blodgett.

"Sorry, no."

"From the East?"

"You could say that, yes, East and somewhat...South," Ms. Starblue appeared to be concentrating hard. I learned that, in this instance, her looks weren't deceiving.

"Well, it is nearly second hour," announced Ms. Blodgett with some ceremony.

She made some general comments and Brian and I filed out with the rest of the class when the bell sounded. There were ten minutes between classes. If I had seen what was coming next...well, I guess I'd have tried to get uncle to drive me back to Montreal.

CHAPTER THREE
Overcome by Almost Everything

"Hey Miller, ya ding-dong!"

It was Justin. He was standing hidden in the bathroom entrance, close to my chipped, grey locker. Dirk McAlester got around on my right. The halls were empty. I was running late, trying to get a chance to inject some heroin. I couldn't help myself. If you've been on drugs...well, you know.

"Brodsky set ya straight?" hissed Dirk. He was a reptile, that one. Not the good kind, either.

"Sure. He said next time, just use bricks."

"You're dead meat, Miller. You gotta know that," Justin told me with something like a growl.

"Get bent."

"We gonna bend you!"

"Looks like you dips didn't learn anything from your last lesson," I said calmly. But my palms were sweating. I prepared to slam my locker closed and book to 2nd hour Science. After smashing the locker door and turning, I found myself nose-to-nose with Derek Peters. All I wanted was a hit of heroin. But waiting resulted in the hit of a fist. One fist, if I were lucky.

"Miller, you're done, you frickin' booger..." said Derek.

A meaty fist rose and flew into my face.

An inch from my nose, another hand came from nowhere.

It caught Derek's knuckles in a vice grip. The catch was made by the skinny, nerdy Ms. Starblue!

"An issue with Mr. Miller, gentlemen?" she demanded quietly. Derek and crew stepped back in surprise.

"This don't concern *you* teach'," said Justin. "Why don't you just step off?"

As quickly as said, Ms. Starblue grabbed both boys pinning me. She lifted them a full two feet off the ground and hurled them into the empty hallway like a couple of bowling balls. I had an unobstructed view and saw that the move cost the thin student teacher almost no effort. Justin Mack was so shocked that a bagel wouldn't cover his gapping yap.

"You'll be late for class, and, dear me, so will your little friends!" she told Justin. And his mouth slammed shut like a trap and the kid took off. The other lunch money-stealers had already disappeared at light speed.

"Wow...lucky for me you came along," said I to Ms. Starblue.

Suddenly I felt very cold. I'll never forget it. The student teacher hadn't turned around. Silence.

She whirled on me with a quickness that was...well, *bizarre*. She got right in my face, the bright, strange eyes flashing fire. I leapt back against my locker. Her green eyes held an irresistible magnetism. She stood a little over me, but seemed larger — much larger. All the relief and gratitude ran out of my face like a punctured tire.

"It wouldn't do to have you harmed…before your time!" said she quietly, staring at me.

"I don't know what you're even talking about."

I smiled at her. She didn't smile back.

Ms. Starblue turned on her heels, and was gone.

II

All day, I noticed Katrina. Our class schedules exactly matched. And the weirdo student teachers shared every class with us, somehow. They seemed to watch the two of us more than anyone else. Not in a good way, either. Finally, school ended and I was heading home, bundled up against the cold, thinking about my part-time job beginning at 5:30 that evening.

"Cat doesn't sit twice on the hot stove, hmm?"

I turned and there was Katrina. She seemed at home in Vermont's weather. We were a block up from Main Street, walking along Fairfield.

"I didn't know Russians knew Irish expressions," I said, taking a wild guess.

I wanted the company. She didn't seem the least bit shy. And never has, so she says.

"I heard about your fight before winter break today. And I happened to see today's little incident with Ms. Starblue."

"You saw that? How? I didn't see anyone around."

"Like way! I was coming around the corner late for our class, too, but you didn't seem to be noticing much. I saw her take those kids off you…pretty wicked, homygod, duh, *score* one for Miller," she send it all awkwardly, with an English accent.

19

"Did you also notice that those new teachers were in all our classes and our schedules are the same?" I said.

"Wicked again, right? Totally TMI."

"TMI?"

"Too much information," said Katrina. "Isn't that one of your idioms, too?"

"One of my what's? TMI is so yesterday! Damn, you Russians talk weird, *geezum crow!*" said I, laughing.

Katrina smiled, embarrassed. "Um, where do you live — and don't swear or you can talk to the hand."

"If you keep walking my way, you'll see," I teased her.

"I'm on Brainerd Street, staying with my Uncle. And you?"

"On Smith Street."

"Rather near you, then, aren't I?"

"Rather?"

"British English. I'm trying to learn American English, can't you tell? And all the happening expressions. Or is it, 'happin' 'spressons — do I got the fly on? But...but I'm not doing well," said she miserably.

"Oh, yes you are, very well!"

"No, I'm not."

"Yes, yes, you are," I said. But she kept up her negative self-talk.

"No. And now you *can* talk to the hand."

"Yes, really!"

And she laughed. It was a loud and long laugh, the kind that makes you smile back.

"You miss Russia."

"Are you asking me or telling me?" she pouted.

"Oh, asking, always asking. You guys have a lady president, right?"

"Uh, we guys do, yes. She is Alexandra Pavelovna Kollanti, a very brilliant woman, but there are so many problems. I worry she will lose her nerve before fixing them. There must be lot of pressure on her."

"Are your parents here in town?"

"Only my Uncle Vanya and his wife live here. My parents are in Montreal. I'll be going there after spring break starts."

"Oh, I thought you were sticking around," I said. She's just temporary, like a foreign exchange student. They come and they go.

"But I'll probably stay the year and visit my parents and my little brother and sister in the spring. My father thinks Saint Albans is the real America."

"Damn, he doesn't get out much."

"He can't give up his old notions," she went on, "but he's very advanced in his thinking—I don't follow most of it, particularly when he gets going. He seems like just a...*buffoon* sometimes—'right word? And no swearing," Katrina said, her light eyebrows knitted.

"Well...maybe."

We reached my house. The driveway called out for shoveling. Katrina re-wrapped her scarf. She was traveling the rest of the quarter mile to her house alone. For a minute, I thought I better offer myself as escort. But I'd pushed it enough with her. And I figured, she'd be leaving, so I kept my distance. That's how it is when you know someone's going to bale.

III

The night was clear and cold. Every star, it seemed, decided to show itself that evening. After work, I turned in early — but nine o'clock found me bolt upright in my bed. And then out of bed and out of our house, too, wide awake.

I saw her coming up Congress Street when I'd reached the base of Har'dack Hill. My Dad's Air Force field jacket still sported staff sergeant stripes.

"Military coat," Katrina said in a sour voice.

"I guess my dad was fighting your country during the Cold War when he wore this."

"Some fight. Who won?"

"It was a draw, right? It got him through college, anyhow," I said, shivering a bit.

"Your dad is home?" she asked.

"No. Well, not here. He skipped out on Moms' while back."

"Oh. Sorry."

"It's okay."

"What brings you out at night like this — it's cold, you know," said Katrina. But I know she didn't think it very cold at all. My wimpy winter, well, it didn't bug the craps out of her, you could just tell.

"No clue. I went to bed early. Something woke me, and here I am!"

"For my part," Katrina answered, "I felt compelled — is that the right word?"

"Yes, ordered, commanded, me too, kind of. I didn't want to put it that way, 'sounds kinda wacky," I said, looking into the woods.

Katrina finished buttoning up her light jacket.

"You Russians sure know how to dress for winter." I'd have frozen to death in that thin, little coat.

"Naturally," the darkness couldn't hide those bright, green eyes.

"Where do we go?"

But she asked, "What do you call this place?"

"Har'dack Hill."

"Weird name. I think…straight into the woods, toward the hill top."

In a much lower voice, I said, "Yeah, I think so, too."

We stole into the tree line, the snowy branches swallowing us up. They wacked themselves back into place behind us. Crime in these parts was rare, so I thought we were safe enough. It wasn't hunting season, which was good. We saw only trees and the glazed by the light of a moon sliver. Minutes of walking revealed lights ahead. Our boots crunched through a layer of ice, making a racket in the silence. Approach unheard would be impossible. Abruptly, a clearing spread before us. We slowly walked out into it, high pines formed a perfect canopy overhead. There were breaks in the branches for the stars to stare down.

Then we saw them.

The light from the distant suns and the moon were enough to make them out. The creatures were huge. There were six, each nearly eight feet tall. Two others stood well apart from main group. All resembled a miniature Tyrannosaurus Rex or perhaps a *velociraptor* from 200 million years ago. But there were some big differences. While their mouths were filled with long, marble colored teeth, the incisors half a foot long, their heads were angular, jaws squared, different from our expectations of a dinosaur-in-miniature. With oval shaped scales overlapping in uniform lines rather than possessed of skin, the creatures had large eyes which stared down lengthy noses. Their bodies looked fit for the most extreme physical combat, revealing nothing of slowness or sloth. We could see that beneath long, flowing robes were chiseled physiques. Their arms where exceptionally defined. This reptilian race had the same number of fingers as us, but tipped with long dagger-like claws. Their bodies were quite proportional; with long legs that look as powerfully built as the rest of them, capable of moving their great weight quickly.

Each head was crowned with a dorsal fin extending upward nearly a foot. These fins cascade down to the end of the tail where they taper. A wide range of color met us, also. Of all the amazing features of the reptilians, the eyes we noticed most. They were clear eyes, and around each iris — and there were two of these — a blue ring appeared to fitfully glowed, two rings of pulsating, bright fire. Two of the creatures were blue — well, 'cerulean' according to Katrina; one was forest green, another one, a shade of blue (okay, 'Baltic' blue, with a brown color extending from the chin all the way along the underside), and finally one of a dark, brownish red (sigh, 'crimson'). The other two, standing almost off the clearing, were each a brownish-blue, one slightly shorter than the other.

We instinctively moved closer together. They moved forward. We forced ourselves to do the same, though my legs were shaking. The aliens each wore a kind of cascading cape and robe of colors ranging from a dark orange to a purple one that was nearly black.

We stopped a few feet from them and they stopped also. The crunching of the snow ended. Silence. Then more moments of quiet but I remember listening to all of us breathing the cold air.

Then without introduction, the creature furthest to the left, took a quick step forward.

The language was not as thickly spoken as we anticipated. It wasn't a hissing, either. Instead, the voice was clear and song-like. We didn't understand any of the individual words, though they were carefully pronounced. But the *meaning of the words* we did understand. The unfamiliar language translated itself into our minds as we listened. It was the oddest sensation — to know the exact meaning of what was said, but not understand the spoken words. I can only liken this to getting a visual image from music, except with all doubt removed. We knew what they were talking about immediately. And it was horrifying.

After the speaker finished, we couldn't reply.

Katrina spoke first, in Russian.

"Excuse me." She gathered herself. "Uh, we understand what you say...but we don't know your language, I guess." She felt helpless and so did I. She was used to dealing with strangers from diplomatic events hosted at the Chakiaya home in Moscow, she told me later. But the creatures before us did not comprehend her. One of the reptilians standing apart jerked its head back at her voice.

"The Universal Language, *Universalian*, is being taught to you. We don't understand *your* languages — yet. But you know the *Universalian* language now. It is an ancient tongue known to all life capable of constructed speech. Apparently you just need some reminding that you know it. It won't take long. Just relax and the words we all understand will come to you, thought and speech."

The speaker sounded patient. The Vermont cold was checked by his calm. We didn't feel anything like a mental transfer underway.

Do you feel any different? Katrina thought, looking at me.

Nope, 'sure don't, I thought back.

Our heads snapped around.

I – I heard, or thought, I mean, what you...thought!

And I hear you. This is...amazing! – but can they hear us? I recall how completely taken I was by this first thought-exchange between Katrina and I.

I don't think they can...unless we address them...

Excuse me, can you hear us? Katrina directed her thoughts at our odd guests.

You're adept now at mental communication. This is a good first step. Relearning Universalian will be easier for you hereafter. If you are willing, Lizardanian and Alligatorian are your next languages to learn.

Sure, we're willing, I thought to them immediately, including Katrina in the direction of my thought – it was like driving a car, just give it a little gas, off you go!

We're not disappointed.

The thoughts were just like voices, but in our minds. Our hearts thumped wildly with anticipation and excitement.

The speaker continued. "The group before you are Lizardanians – Ettoros, Loridian, Direidian, Korillia, and Urielian and over here we have Danillia and Soreidian." The other two did not exchange a friendly thought but just glared coldly. The pair standing apart seemed interested in being elsewhere. Their huge hands rested on the hilts of swords worn at their sides; long, entirely black swords. They were of an odd design. These two looked positively sulking and angry.

"And I am Torrillian," the speaker continued. Snow began falling faster. The pine canopy only allowed a few flakes to find their way down.

"The Twins of Triton are coming to destroy your world, as I told you a moment ago. There is nothing that Lizardania can do. It's the natural course of your evolution. We are here to arrange the removal of thirty young people — and the two of you. The Thirty are already chosen. We have reason to believe they will leave voluntarily. This gesture is more than your race deserves according to some of us," and he looked over at the two standing apart. Danillia and Soreidian appeared to be the only ones armed. With their long obsidian blades, they seemed even more intimidating, if that were possible.

"But that much will be done. In our estimation, you have about twenty-three revolutions around your sun left. Maybe less given that the Twins will speed up as they close in. You will meet us here tomorrow night, saying what goodbyes you will before then, and we will depart. First we will go to Alligatoria to meet Littorian, the Lord of the Lizardanians (or so he is called on such occasions). Then you will come to Lizardania."

To Katrina and me, the hard-hearted announcements felt like being hit in the face with an ice ball.

"Bring nothing with you," he went on, ignoring our shocked expressions. "All will be provided. And now, that's done. So I believe the proper wish is…"

and the Lizardanian then actually attempted some English.

"...good night!"

Satisfied with that, the miniature dragons simply turned away and started walking toward their small, sleek starships. Danillia and Soreidian, however, stepped into the woods apparently on another course.

Katrina let them go a few paces before she cried in *Universalian,*

"Wait! Please wait!"

She was quicker with the language than I. The six turned nearly in unison, their reptilian features emotionless. The two that went into the woods returned.

"Is there something else?" asked Torrillian matter-of-factly. "What have I forgotten?" Torrillian said, looking to his fellows. Danillia and Soreidian looked totally torqued. Their long, clawed hands hadn't left their sword hilts.

"Yes, there is...there is something else," I said. I thought fast and looked at my friend, who was also thinking hard. "We need to talk to your, ah...superiors, please."

A little rumble began among the aliens. Laughter!

"You will soon discover more about us as your minds become accustomed to our way of learning. This is a process that should be very exciting for you. Later you'll learn why Lizardanians have no...*superiors*...accept in special times, such as these."

"We need a moment before you leave...if you will," said Katrina, saving the day again.

"We'll wait...if...you have the time."

Katrina whirled on me at that strange reply and we both started talking simultaneously, in our newly learned mental language and in noisome English, French and Russian, neither of us got a word in edgewise. Finally I thought to her,

Look, just think what's on your mind, one thing at a time.

Fine, fine…but they might be able to hear us like this, don't you think? It's something they've taught us to do, after all!

I don't think so. They seem too…classy for eve's dropping, I speculated.

Brian, what'll we do?

Well…let's try to be cool. Maybe we misheard them. I felt desperate and I was sweating.

We'd better say something…and fast.

They can't expect us to go with them and leave everyone!

No. No we can't…I have some questions before they just go traipsing off!

Katrina cleared her throat.

"Excuse me again. But could you please tell us something about these, ah, Twins of Triton, that are supposedly coming to kill everyone?" she attempted to mask it, but I could tell Katrina was afraid.

Torrillian walked to within a couple feet of us, crunching loudly through the frozen snow and hidden pine needles. When they first get up on you, they're…well, it's just amazing.

"It is not *supposedly*, young one, *it is a certainty.* About 65 million years ago, by your star system's time, life on your planet was almost all destroyed. Before that, 250 million years ago, a similar event occurred. The impact of the earlier comet was an immediate extinction-level event, plunging your world into 400 years of darkness and freezing temperatures. The galaxy is a violent place—worlds

29

come and they go. Only 10 million years ago, ash destroyed what dinosaurs were left here. As you see, planetary destruction is natural. The second asteroid, by the way, did not kill quite ALL life on this world — hence your people being here at all. This new comet-event, will be the most destructive ever. It is actually a binary asteroid — two comets locked in gravitational attraction. It would be a beautiful spectacle if the results weren't predestined to be so…um, *unpleasant*. Planets come and now it is time for yours to go."

"Can't you stop these comets?" I asked. I couldn't believe how unconcerned this creature seemed.

"I can't stop the Twins," was Torrillian's icy response.

Fortunately, Katrina thought about the answer.

"But could *your people*, or maybe *your friends*, if they wanted to?"

It was apparently a good question, for the aliens immediately conferred. Katrina sounded diplomatic, dancing around our fear of a flat walk-out by the reptilians.

They are about WAY cool, thought I to Katrina, unable to control my admiration. No one could have. I have done no justice to their appearance. They're something you have to see.

'Way! They're…magnificent — but are they kind…or cold?

You mean in the way that, you know, reptiles are cold-blooded?

I mean in the way that they'll just let our people die! And that's everything alive on this world, you know, Brian, not just humans. How can they permit it?

I dunno. We're going to find out…we permit a lot of death on this planet that we can prevent, don't we? But I didn't want to argue too hard for our limitations, certainly not right then.

Torrillian came back.

"Lizardanians are not particularly war-like, at least not anymore. We have precious few space vessels with the kind of firepower necessary to confront the Twins. It would be very difficult to bring all these ships together. It is conceivable that together with Lizardania's friends the Twins might be defeated, but I doubt Lizardania would make such an unusual request, certainly not on your behalf. These asteroids are different from the last that came here. They are moving faster, thrown out of their orbit around Neptune's moon, Triton, with tremendous gravitational force. They aren't just going to wander into this world. And they are composed of an exceptionally dense metal. Most formidable. Stopping them would be essentially impossible."

Then Torrillian looked down on us apologetically; wear his eyebrows sound be, he looked sad.

"Even if the motivation to try to stop the comets existed within Lizardania, our weapons wouldn't be enough. Also, the fact that the collision course is so exact — we anticipate impact between — what is it? — your northern Africa and Europe. Many of our people believe this to be the natural course of events in your evolutionary cycle. It wouldn't be right to interfere with the planetary life cycle."

"Extinction's natural? And you said 'essentially' — what's that mean?" I asked. Katrina shot me a warning look.

"You humans have brought your species, and others, to the brink of extinction, on your own, correct? Don't you think this happens in the galaxy? Understand that collisions are natural in planetary formation. Many stars have seen their offspring die over the eons."

"Couldn't you…help us destroy the Twins? We have weapons, some big ones. We have hundreds, thousands of missiles, you see, that we built for a war you should give us credit for never fighting."

Torrillian appeared unmoved.

"You have them…now. The asteroids are locked gravitationally, between Neptune and Earth. Like a weather stream, they follow a fixed course. As to friends who can help, while the possibility exists, the motivation does not. The time is too short."

We demand to speak to those who would save us. Katrina was indignant in her thought to Torrillian.

Lizardania is represented before you.

Why won't you help?

Humanity isn't worth saving.

You're wrong — you don't know us.

We know enough.

Katrina turned to me. We were so close together, mostly out of fear, our heads were nearly touching.

Go for the top guy.

"We want to talk to Littorian about why you should help our world." Katrina told them very loudly, in *Universalian.*

"It's clear to us that you wish to Present. Do you wish to Present?"

At that, Katrina and I did a double-take, but we said nothing.

"You may Present tomorrow. Meet us here on this spot at…" and he looked at a device he pulled from a belt worn under his long, layered cloak. That clothing alone, overlapping in design like shingles on a house, seemed all the creatures needed to protect themselves from the freezing Vermont night. Later we learned they didn't even need that.

"...nine o'clock in the evening. Yes, that's the time. We will take you somewhere on your world and from there we will entertain your Presentation on the worth of humanity — and why it should be saved. And we will tell you why you're wrong. During the spectacle, which will last until morning touches this hill, and on this hill only, we will listen to you both — to you two alone. At the encounter's end, you'll be brought back here to continue with your daily lives until next evening. For children of this time and place, that means going to school, which is good, for you both have much to learn. We should not interrupt that learning process."

He stopped a moment and eyed Danillia and Soreidian, with a little saber-tooth-flashing grin.

"In between Presentations, we will bring your message to those who would listen. You will not, after the first meeting, be permitted to eat or sleep, for you will be Presenting. These rules are strict, old, almost as old as the Beginning, and cannot be changed. To Present to Lizardania is a ceremony of highest honor — it is rarely suffered. It is only because Littorian thought you might ask that we entertain your request now. He is wise and can see things well in advance. I am always amazed at his gifts. Will you speak or will you sing to us?"

At first we weren't sure we'd understood the question. So we didn't say anything.

The snow fell through the pines. The Lizardanians looked like they had all the time in the world. But we didn't. We knew *time* was now our one, true enemy.

Katrina looked blankly at me.

Sing? What's he mean? thought she.

Hmmm…not sure. You play instruments, right?

Lots, yes.

Guitar?

Yes; in my homeland, I play the balalaika, and electrical guitar — so what?

I looked at the Lizardanians.

We'd better sing. If we just debate them, somehow I think we'll be cut to pieces. They know the language, we're just learning. They're waiting.

But Brian, what will we sing about?

We'll think of something later. I know you worry we'll make fools of ourselves. But it's something they'll respect more, I can feel it. The other road isn't any good.

"We will sing to you," said Katrina with finality. "Only…we don't know what kind of music…you like to listen to…" The Russian felt like walking into an unfamiliar, darkened room, groping for a light switch she couldn't find.

"We will provide you instruments. You already know what music to sing, Katrina. You will teach Brian and we will listen to you both."

Just then, Torrillian turned to Danillia and Soreidian. Obviously there was a fierce mental discussion going on between them. The two angry-looking Lizardanians squeezed their sword hilts so firmly that we heard what sounded like leather being ripped. Finally Torrillian turned back to us. "You will only drink Lizardanian water — you will find it refreshing and energizing, which you will need. When you wish to stop singing to us and when you ask us for a final answer, it will be over. Each night you will know what Lizardania has thought of your music — for we will answer in music and song. Your world will watch."

"Excuse me, Torrillian," I said. "Our world won't understand—"

"But it will," snapped another of the Lizardanians, the Baltic one. "Your governments with the ability to observe space already know of the Twins—and their course. They hold the knowledge. This makes something less than a positive impression about you," it was the one introduced as Direidian.

"But when people see us, wherever you take us...to...to Present," Katrina chimed in, her voice rising as it did when she grew agitated, "they won't allow us to return each night because...because they won't understand."

I added, "Our families could get in trouble, too. People won't get it. They'll probably just...freak out."

Torrillian considered.

"You will be clothed in Lizardanians garments. Over your heads, we will provide you a kind of mask. Something hooded—yes, we can produce that. Your voices will be unimpeded but unfamiliar to your people since you'll use our languages. As to whether your people 'freak out,' that is now another of *your* problems. These clothes will be here tomorrow night. They will belong to you, to take where you will. And these are yours, also," the Lizardanian walked quickly for some one so big. For both of us, he placed a silver chain over our heads. From each chain, there was a silver ornament. The shape of the little object was, it still seems to me, an upside-down sailboat. After a moment we realized that shape was roughly that of the ships that waited for the Lizardanians there in the snow.

Katrina and I wanted to talk and plan, but Torrillian was speaking again.

"Your minds will soon be drinking from the vast—you will think bottomless—lakes of our knowledge. The struggle will be a fair one. We will listen to your music. You, Katrina will tell us why humanity should survive given what your race knows of the sciences, of mathematics and of the stars. If you prove capable of learning, that may help your case. But I doubt it," and at that Katrina audibly sucked her teeth, something I figure she learned at our school.

"You, Brian Miller," Torrillian went on, taking no notice, "in your music will tell us about the history of your people. You'll explain why they merit something that I have never seen given to another race: Interference with nature's course. You have some, shall we say, 'personal challenges' to overcome. Perhaps you will—but, again, I doubt it, on both points. We know something of this race already. After you begin to Present, if you consume sustenance beyond Lizardanian water or if you sleep, we will consider your case completed. We will then decide on what we have heard. I will tell Littorian of all we have agreed to."

He had given us a fair chance—NOT!

"Finally," he said, "I advise you...*to be cautious.* Your people may find you before you have finished Presenting. And they will be looking for you after the first night of Presentation. Also, I think you err in wishing to Present with music. You will both *fall.*"

Without a further word of departure, explanation, farewell, and definitely not encouragement, the Lizardanians left for their ships. They were gone, and the clearing echoed with a slight humming, the small ships flashing through the canopy. Danillia and Soreidian strode away into the woods. We quickly lost sight of them. The idea that those two were wondering around our neighborhood only added to our feelings of creeping panic. Above, the stars looked down, the cat's whisker of moon having lengthened. And also there was *one star* that we noticed, one that looked very bright—but not beautiful. Not beautiful at all.

IV

We walked back down the hill. The task seemed too hopeless to even discuss.

"I can't believe this is really happening..." said Katrina.

"Yeah...boy, like...score! You're in a lot of trouble."

"Say what?"

"I'm kidding. *WE'RE...in a LOT...*of trouble."

"That's better. I still can't believe...I must be asleep! You've something to overcome? How's that?"

I had to tell her. I couldn't even look up, I was so ashamed of my weakness, and of letting her down. So I just spoke to the snow, quickly.

"Katrina...I haven't told you something about me. I've been taking drugs, these last couple of weeks. Heroin. I need more. Soon, too—I can't cope without it. Some dude got me on it, I didn't even see this guy, the dealer. He sold me my hits in an alley downtown. It was dark. Sorry I didn't tell you. I'm having...I think they call it withdrawal symptoms. I'm shaking a lot...and some other stuff I don't want to talk about."

She was silent as we walked along.

I bit my lower lip. I so hated to admit it. I felt like I was betraying her. The drug had taken hold of me, there was nothing like it. It was a part of me. At that time, I couldn't imagine even one more night without the stuff.

"Okay...we'll fight both the drugs and the aliens together. You have to give it up, the world depends on it, Brian Miller. If you need treatment, you're going to get it. You're going through rehab with me, right here and now. There is no one to help me but you. Understand? Do I sound bossy now? My friends back home say I am. Oh, I'm sorry." She was nice about it, but she *is* a pushy thing.

Of course, I knew she was right—about everything.

"I want to be done with it," I told her, now looking at her smooth face. She has high cheekbones which are always rosy, probably all that exposure to harsh winters. "Sure, we've hurt our planet...and ourselves. It's obvious. But we've done a lot of good, too. I'm going to tell them so."

"I'll be with you, Brian—until the end."

"Sleep in tomorrow's my advice," I sighed, and stopped walking. "That's our last shut-eye."

We stopped in the snow.

"I knew there was something wrong. But you can beat this, Brian. I'll help you."

"Yeah."

"It's a stupid ritual, no food, no sleep? What kind of 'Presenting' can you do when you're tired and hungry?"

"Lots of rituals are stupid. They don't want us to last long."
"Show up late to school, huh?"

"Your English is changing into American fast," I told her; and it was.

"Good night, Brian Miller, sleep well. Don't worry. We'll wake up and it will have been a bad dream...and a good one in parts, I guess. They were... *cool.* You wouldn't be bugged by loser Justin and his friends with one of *them*! It sure felt real. Wouldn't it be *totally rad* if they were real...but the Twins weren't?"

"Yeah. But they sound like a package set. Everything good in my life has something bad attached." I headed up to my door. I no longer felt even slightly warm.

CHAPTER FOUR
Let Us Not Go Gently

I

It was 9:00 a.m. I lay in bed. I'd figured I was sleepwalking. A few choice words to Mom on the edge of sleep permitted extra time after she first woke me. I knew that the night before with Katrina had been a dream. She'd just made such a strong impression on me. Even walking home with her was probably part of the dream. Wanting to kiss her, well, that was more like a fantasy.

Jumping up, I went to the window. I make sure to put down my right foot down first when I get out of bed—kinda superstitious thing. There was snow everywhere, of course, but it was a sunny day, just the same. The light reflected off the snow so strong that you couldn't look at it. I put my hand over my eyebrows. I looked into the light blue sky. Nope, no asteroids barreling down on my icy world.

Asteroids — OhhmyGauudd! Who's clueing out now?

I stared at the Superman clock by my bed stand. It was a neat clock, 'got it in Canada, *next door.* The dream was over, I was two hours late for school—

another, unhappy first. Then I remembered the
ornament from the dream. Proof of memory or
fantasy would be hanging from my neck. At first I
didn't reach…then I grabbed at my chest, dreading it.

And it was there.

I'll never forget how I felt, holding that ornament.
There was a roaring in my ears—and raw panic. A
hundred visions of a very dark future hit me, like a
blade. I thought about the death that would be
visited on the Earth when the Twins came—and went,
maybe, tearing though Earth. It would be like a bullet
flying through a human body. Two big bullets. My
body ached, then, for heroin. I dropped to my knees
at the thought of the drug racing through my veins
again—and how it could wash away the
responsibility that hung around my neck. I went
downstairs.

"Lunch money check? You'll need this note, too,"
Mom said, as I pulled on coat, gloves, hat, scarf and
backpack in nearly a single movement. That's a
Vermont trait, putting on more than one thing at a
time.

"Oh, yeah, forgot…"

"What's got you preoccupied, hon? Are you
sick?"

"Do I look sick, Ma?"

"You look great, hon."

"So do you, Ma. Thanks for the extra sleep.
'Love ya!" and I was gone, like the winter wind
sweeping me off the snowy porch.

I kicked through the heavy, white sea. I looked
for Katrina. I looked down at yesterday's footprints.
It seemed a long time ago, and I wasn't sure they
were the footprints of two teens on a special, well, *the
most special*, mission ever. I stopped, staring down.

"Those're old," it was Katrina coming up behind. I still gapped at the footprints.

"So it happened."

"Sure, what'd you think? Like a Shakespearian play, something just made-up?"

"I thought Shakespeare was based on real life."

"Oh, I know. It's neither. It's the last history play, Brian. 'Got one of those sailboats?'"

"Yeah," I told her quietly. "I do."

"Me, too."

"You thought it was a dream," I said.

"You're asking me or telling me?"

"You can't read my thoughts?"

"I see things, images — they must be your thoughts, and the thoughts of others, too — people different from us. Different even from them...it's kind of creepy," Katrina then looked up into the clear sky. Soon it would be cloudy, as it became often enough during the day, this far north. In the evenings, the clouds would clear, making for orange, red or purple sunsets.

School was about a half mile distant, and we were getting closer fast.

"You're scared?" I asked her. I sure was.

"I know I look it..."

I spoke Russian back to her, which made her jump.

"Strange to have someone else in my head like this. It's somehow...empowering. And your language isn't all I'm learning...there are three others, at least," I said.

"I feel them, too...it's like being in three classrooms at once — four counting the School of Brian."

Please ignore all the bad words you might find in my nasty attic.

It's okay. I'm still intent on breaking you of the habit.

Good luck — which one?

We'll need it — and all the bad ones.

You got a note for being late?

Yup. You?

Yup, and didn't even have to forge it!

Into the old school building and straight to third hour we went, after a quick checking-in with a surly Front Office staff. Our notes earned us a hall pass. We went off to History, with Mr. Triassic teaching.

We tried to enter quietly, and did, from the back of the classroom. But Mr. Triassic was having none of it.

"Well everyone look at who's finally here! We're honored that you could find time in your busy personal schedules to attend school," Mr. Triassic said to us, making us scramble awkwardly to our desks. Some kids laughed at us, the way it always happens when the teacher nails someone. It sucks.

We sat and looked to the front.

Then we saw those eyes.

Katrina and I looked at each other. No wonder they went into the woods last night, and not in their ships. On the instant, the two of us knew that this was not a student teacher from the University of Vermont. We were looking at a Lizardanian, one who would be hammering us that very night, somewhere on our planet, 9 o'clock sharp.

The Mr. Triassic who wasn't Mr. Triassic but something more, stared back.

He could tell that we recognized him. But he smiled toward the class anyway. He didn't have a care in the doomed-world.

"Ready to join us?" asked the student teacher in a mocking, cold voice.

For Katrina and I, he was talking about something more than today's lesson.

I felt immediately a series of disturbances in my mind, very unusual thoughts in a day of wild, flying, distorted ideas — silent and stern — something was offended. I glanced at Katrina and saw a look of defiance, a hurt and righteous glare, directed at Mr. Triassic. It matched the one Ms. Starblue had after saving me from Justin and his flunkies...

Ms. Starblue...

I knew Katrina would confront Mr. Triassic match him insult for dangerous insult. Quick to judge, quick to anger — maybe it was a Russian thing.

*Don't do it, Kat, that's what they want, to wear you down here where it doesn't count — save it for tonight. Rest now, don't fight...*I thought it to her hard, maybe just a voice in the wilderness — but she heard. She started...then looked to me.

I hear you.

Do you?

They make me so mad.

We mess this up, everyone dies. Really.

You're right...not a word...until tonight...then it's in song! The words are already coming to me.

Way cool. Don't waste words now. You'll be fighting for everyone who has ever lived...and everybody that's ever died trying.

Mr. Triassic turned back to the board, giving us an unintended reprieve to gather our thoughts. We'd interrupted the lesson at hand.

"So we can conclude that your — the — First World War was waged to determine which elites would control emerging world markets and the colonies harnessed, shall we say, (I think we shall!) to that purpose. And what quote did I recently see? The Third World War will be fought with nuclear weapons and the Fourth World War you'll—er, *we'll*—fight with clubs, eh? Would you agree with that Mr. Miller, or was it all something about making the world safe for democracy, the First World War, I mean?"

I felt like I'd been slapped with a frying pan. Apparently there would be no reprieve until that evening if this Lizardanian had anything to say about it. The class awaited my answer with some audible amusement, snickering and incessant teeth sucking.

I tried to be equal to the moment.

"War's accelerated social change, my Dad always told me. To boil it all down to just one cause rips off the sacrifice of millions of people, dead and living. So I don't think you really get it, at all."

The class hesitated in its response. My enemies snickered, my fans looked from one to another to see who'd understood the reply. Fortunately, as I finished, the bell rang to signal the end of Third Hour and the beginning of the little ten minute break between classes—between duels it now appeared to Katrina and I.

"Well," said Mr. Triassic with a grin, "Off to your next class. Thank you for an enlightening discussion."

All the students rose and we with them. We began shuffling out, everything returning to normal, laughing and talking about everything and making light of anything. Some whispered about the new, nutty professor.

"Not you, Ms. Chakiaya. Neither you, Mr. Miller—a word about your tardiness! Could you close the door Ms. Dullsaliere, if you please? Thanks, this won't take two minutes," and he took a seat behind his desk, the picture of relaxed nonchalance, his old clothing and too-short tie simply a ridiculous, comic sight. The door closed, with Janel Dullsaliere smiling back at me as if to say, 'You're busted, rock star!' We stopped heading for the door and just sat down side-by-side. In this classroom, there were long tables chairs under them. In some classes the chairs and the desks were one unit, but not here.

The door closed and the old latch sounded. It sounded like the hammer of a gun being cocked. Mr. Triassic suddenly bounded over the teacher's desk, with inhuman agility. He landed just in front of Katrina. Other than the whack of his hands on the desk, he made no more noise than a house cat.

Talk about freaked-out, boy I was!

Mr. Triassic bent down. But to my complete amazement, Katrina moved not at all, but seemed ready for this intimidation. The student teacher then backed away and on the spot, Mr. Triassic melted before us like a candle burning in fast motion, wax evaporating into something entirely different from the tweed-jacketed, awkward Mr. Triassic. Before us stood a Lizardanian, robbed, but at least without a sword.

"I'm Soreidian. We met last night," and the colossal creature was even more intimidating in full daylight. I nearly crapped myself, to be honest about it.

"Where's your sword at?" I forced myself to say, rudely. "Don't you feel safer with that?"

Katrina and I were wrestling with a mix of admiration, naked fear, a longing to befriend the creature before us, one who had the power to allow

47

life to exist on Earth—*or not*. A powerful desire to see
the stars that had produced such a magical beast,
seized us both. We fought to control ourselves,
nearly carried away by the strength, the majesty of
the creature before us. It's a wild feeling. You can
actually sense the warmth, the energy rolling off of
them. As the classroom's eight windows filled the
room with rare winter sunlight, we could appreciate
the amazing, statuesque being.

"Everything's eventually, Mr. Miller."

Soreidian strode about the room, a long tail
carefully guided, so as not to make splinters out of
every desk and chair. The creature might have been a
cross between an Allisaurous and a Raptor tearing
through some rift in time. But it was different from
any dinosaur or dragon we had ever encountered in
bedtime tales.

"Soon, though, your minds will fully encounter
the thought of my race. It's something that I
personally detest. But I know it's being done. I
know…that you're training. So are The Thirty, but
not nearly as extensively as you two. This is
happening because you somehow convinced a few of
my people that a hearing is due you. Make the case,
you say, that your world is worth saving? I, for one,
believe you can't. And so you *must* fall."

The icy words really bothered us. But we knew,
too, what hung in the balance.

"I was told about this, um, *development*, only
recently," went on the Lizardanian, standing back
with his massive arms folded across his scaled chest.

"I am not delighted to be here. While I've studied
something of your race, transmissions and radio
waves and have to a degree an understanding of
Brian's language at least, I still have many questions.

And *Russian*…is too much for me, what a complicated, bothersome language! It is much harder than Brian's and I reject it. What possible good can it do me to learn more than one of these stupid human languages? I might agree that the race merits thirty of its youth to be saved, perhaps the two of you also, but nothing else. You," and he turned on me, "will be my opponent, it seems, in an effort to remind my race that yours is a failed experiment. Your people are hardly worthy of the tremendous effort and possible endangerment of many of our own to destroy the Twins. It's especially arrogant of you," the Lizardanian's voice was raspy and reptilian, now sounding more like what we would have expected from someone who looked like him. *Universalian* was very different in tone when spoken—there was no song in the voice we heard now.

"Our people," went on the Soreidian, "are debating the role we should play in helping other races. In my opinion—"

Katrina boldly interrupted the lecture.

"—Fortunately your opinion isn't the only one," her hands were folded, but I knew the palms were damp.

The Lizardanian narrowed the distance between himself and Katrina, invading her personal space again. Hot, breath accompanied by the scent of—*burning roses*. In Katrina's mind, this scent was recalled, and I could feel her thinking about it, trying to place it. It was in Russia, …a long time ago. Not unpleasant, we didn't back away. Then we both felt sleepy. It was a pleasant, almost hypnotic drowsiness. We both violently shook our heads and shoved our chairs back. Sleep was our enemy now.

"You'll find us frighteningly independent. Frightening...even to me," said Soredian, now backing off. "Without my help, you'll have little chance against the Twins. And I tell you now, Ms. Chakiaya, nothing you *sing*, nothing you *say* and nothing you *think* will convince me to help your primitive and under-civilized race! Now go, the both of you, lest you be late...*for class!*" There stood the nerdy, but lumbering Mr. Triassic, the waxen image now restored. I noticed a slight look of strain on his disguised face—then it was gone.

Mr. Triassic went back to the front of the class, roughly rummaging through the schedule book on the teacher's desk. "I have seen other worlds more deserving than this be destroyed—without our interference. And I don't feel guilty about it. But helping your world in the face of that history *would* make me feel guilty. Natural courses, the selection of which races rise and fall, is not the domain of Lizardania nor our friends. Your planet has seen extinction before, it will know it again. Now, get out." The door rattled.

"Oh, too bad. I detained you through break! Ms. Starblue does not like to be kept waiting. I believe the full time teacher in physical education has allowed her to teach today. I hope she doesn't wear you out," he added the last with a curious, very human wink, a self-satisfied grin across his wide, plastic face.

We moved quickly to go.

"One last thing, if you please," said Mr. Triassic, as I had the door knob in hand. "If both or either of you will walk away from this—just renounce your intentions to sing to us—I will personally save you both and even your entire families—I'll personally move them from this planet—an answer, please?"

"What about our people?" I asked.

"It must be left to nature, Mr. Miller. The course of the asteroids is in a line with your orbit around this sun. That can't be helped. These asteroids were in orbit around Triton. They were dislodged, well, naturally enough. They will hit your planet—naturally. To interfere is defilement of science and of the order of the galaxy. Can't your little human minds understand that?"

"This world's fate should be with you in it," said Katrina solemnly.

The student teacher made a sour face. "Impossible."

"No deal, then," I told him, actually snapping my fingers, which isn't like me. He just pissed me off so bad!

Mr. Triassic wore a piteous expression. "My offer remains, in spite of your insolence," said Soreidian—and went back to his papers. "You will find me less recriminatory than a human given the same discourteous reply," he added, bitingly.

The door rattled again, with students trying to enter.

"Lizardanian water is refreshing and even nourishing. But it is all you may consume until Lizardania has reached its decision—the same for myself and Starblue. And there is to be no sleeping on any of our parts—we're all being monitored—"

"—How?" interrupted Katrina.

"I won't tell you," growled the student teacher, this time actually snapping his own fingers, mimicking me. Only Mr. Triassic's fingers snapping sounded like a gunshot, making us jump.

I opened the door to leave, the click-clack this time reminding me of a bolt on a machine gun being

51

pulled back.

"Perhaps a few days without food or sleep will awaken you...to the realities of your situation," whispered Mr. Triassic.

"Hey, no worries, man," I told him.

We left the door open.

CHAPTER FIVE
In the War Place

The hours flew toward 9:00 p.m. In the little border town of Saint Albans, Vermont, a place not too many people knew about, Brian Miller and I rested in our respective beds. We didn't dare sleep. We stared up at our ceilings. And at a quarter to nine, we both rose, like the dead summoned from catacombs. Our minds bridged the distance between us and we planned our evening. We donned our coats and winter things stashed outside, so as not to alert adults. We met on the snow-covered road, near Har'dack Hill.

"Are you ready, Katrina?" Brian asked me.

"*Neht*," I told him.

"Well, let's just go anyhow. It's only going to change the whole world, no big deal. It's scheduled to get wasted anyway."

"Da — no biggie, right? Thanks for framing it positively for me, 'needed that," so I punched him playfully in the shoulder.

"Ouch," he squealed — yes, he squealed and I'm leaving that in, because it's the truth, he can be such a panzie! "Damn, you Russian girls hit hard, or is that something they've taught you?"

It was a clear night again, which made it colder. The stars were exceptionally bright, the moon a slender crescent, only a little thicker than last night.

"Sorry, 'didn't mean to hurt you. And don't swear. It's demeaning."

"Hands?"

In the available moonlight, I smiled.

"You need to hold my hand, Brian Miller? Is this an official date?" I said it in Russian to challenge him. But it took Brian no time to translate the words.

"Well, not yet...I'll ask you when this is over. For now, maybe we can just, you know, hold hands, if you can take being with a kid of my reputation," he did well with Russian, I was impressed. This mode of learning would also change the world, if we could share it, if there was world left to share it with.

"Well, stick with me. I'll keep you out of trouble. The principal already told you not to cheat when you fight."

"How do you know that? Besides, he said don't fight at all. If so much wasn't, you know, at stake, you can be sure I wouldn't."

"But since so much *is* at stake?"

"Well, I love my family. I'll fight, and we have to win...by any means necessary. More depends on it than just humans."

"You're right. And yes, hold my hand. And they said they'd save the families if we surrender. And what do you mean by any means necessary?"

"Kat," and he looked me in the eyes. "I mean what I say."

"Does that apply to anyone in trouble? Do the ends justify the means, Brian?"

He thought about it, and then he looked up at the sky.

"Tonight they do." And his glove and my mitten collided.

I

Before us stood all eight Lizardanians—Torrillian, Ettoros, Direidian, Korillia, Urielian, Loridian, Soreidian and Danillia. This time we easily recognized the last two as being the student teachers. Their cold looks and the unique faces of chiseled, scaled granite told us we were unwelcome. Reptilian in appearance, they would be 'dragon-men,' 'dinosaur-men,' or 'lizard-men,' or 'star-lizards' or something equally stupid to a shocked world, once seen.

I didn't know what to do about those perceptions and neither did Brian. We'd just have to endure whatever people came up with. Brian feared what the media would do to them. It might be pretty hard to stereotype the Lizardanians, each had a unique identity and they governed themselves with an amazing independence. What would the world do with such images? Brian thought of a million web pages full of silliness and shallow commentary, and I shuttered at his thought.

We attempted to be on our best behavior. We both bowed before the group. But the Lizardanians, at this gesture, exchanged quizzical expressions.

Opps, that was dumb, they don't bow, thought I.

They don't have leaders, remember? I guess no one answers to anyone else. Wow, what would that be like? Brian thought back.

'Sounds like chaos.
'Sounds like freedom.
'Chaos.
'Freedom!
Try to get some fries just on freedom.
Brian smiled at me.
You're really changing into an American on me.
Like, talk to the hand!
Torrillian spoke.

"The instruments will be there when you arrive. There are your garments. These were made by the Seree race. They are great gifts to you. When you wear the headdress, you will be unidentifiable. You will still be able to see each, by the way. You will reintegrate into your normal school day tomorrow. And we would suggest to your people that they continue to live their normal lives unchanged, after they recover from the shock of seeing and hearing you tonight. That is, *if* they ever do! And it wouldn't do for you to miss school just because your world is coming to an end."

I looked to Brian, and we tried to figure whether the Lizardanian was serious. Since Torrillian was at least pretending to be, we accepted the words without question.

We felt our blood racing and music flowed into our minds. The music of our spirits, becoming available, to be tapped in several languages, to draw on like batteries—it was ours. Strange instruments to sing the words were now instantly familiar to us, learned now from ancient knowledge when the stars were younger, life more vibrant, and voices never lost. We felt suddenly prepared. This was the mother of all exams.

"Danillia and I believe they should NOT be

dressed in the garments of the Seree!" interjected Soreidian angrily, the gift a total surprise to him.

The other six Lizardanians turned to regard the two part-time student teachers.

"Littorian will be here soon, you can take it up with him—after all, this IS a special time! I believe it was the Seree's idea. They knew the Presenters wanted to remain anonymous, to die with their people. And you know their failure is a certainty."

That's a little premature.

I agree, we're not done yet, not by a long shot, Brian responded excitedly.

Not-Mr. Triassic and Not-Ms. Starblue glared at us, but did not raise the issue again.

I stepped forward, Brian by my side.

Hanging before us, at the edge of the clearing, hovering chest high to a Lizardanian, were two beautiful costumes. The robes were graceful; flowing capes were somehow built-in. The headdress, a cross between mask and helmet, but constructed in cascading patterns which overlapped like a waterfall, each tier blending in to the one beneath it. It reminded me of the scales on our hosts. We reached out and nothing more pleasant ever crossed our fingers. It was like the smoothest leather, yet firm at the same time. In the cold air, the garments were pleasantly warm and compelled us to throw aside convention and modesty and don them on the spot.

"You will wear these for our first encounter. After dressing, we will be off. Your people will see you—and us. It will change your world, as you can imagine. You must prepare yourselves. There may be some turmoil on your world, but it might be a comfort for you to know that without your effort, nothing would have changed anyway. And again, that's your problem," said Direidian, eyeing us closely.

Brian and I were experiencing an epiphany of knowledge and foreign thoughts which completely and without control flooded our minds. These new thoughts, at first a trickle of a babbling brook, then a stream, and now a rushing river, were drowning us in a ferocious torrent, a tsunami of learning. We felt...purified, cleaned, lifted up above the everyday problems of a teenager, better than we were, but still human, with all our failings unfortunately intact.

In moments, we were dressed. The sleeves hung in a wide mouth below our hands, warming our arms. There were gloves and boots. A tighter, inner material covered our arms down to the wrists. Finally we turned to our hosts with solemn resolution—we had a world to save. We were dressed to do it. We placed the hooded helmet-masks over our heads. These were angular looking and gave us a fierce appearance. But I wouldn't know how fierce until I saw ourselves on TV.

"Where do we go and how?" asked Brian.

A small ship, as if summoned, glided into view from the direction of Congress Street. It was utterly silent in its approach. The lighted streets were darkened as the craft arrived. It made its way into the clearing within the woods of Har'dack Hill. Geometrical, angled, the craft stood some ten feet high and double that across. It resembled a polygon and a doorway revealed itself to us.

"Aboard, please," said Loridian.

When the last Lizardanian stood in the interior, with Brian and I beside them, the doorway was filled as though never there.

It was very dark when we arrived with the Lizardanians at the Pentagon in Washington, D.C.

II

The shock across the country and the world was total and nearly instantaneous. A message sent at Internet speed, with such powerful implication, filled the planet with a silent awe. From Peking to Buenos Aires, the world learned two small spacecraft loitered amongst the trees of the Pentagon's Center Courtyard. Our world learned in shocked quiet that two more such ships waited motionlessly above the gray building like sentinels. Billions of wide eyes drank up the wild images, images that Brian and I were at least used to by now. Billions, of course, were used to similar images from movies, books, and their imaginations. But in real life, we feared it would be too much for people. But chaos did not result—only silence. As though a thousand years of speculation about alien beings had done its work, people looked now upon the scene, realizing that the day of contact had finally arrived.

Brian and I stood anonymously and quietly on the circular road that lined the interior of the Pentagon. This little road circled the pleasant courtyard and the trees and beautiful landscaping around us mocked the hellish place responsible for the killing of countless humans. Here, many a troubled mind had gathered its nerve in the building's wooded interior, and after a break, returned to do their foul deeds against their own kind. I did not envy Brian his task at that moment.

Overcoming our history was, as someone had recently put it, his problem.

For those few people aware of the Twins, it was a double shock. For these few, the connection between the two events was established immediately.

A slight breeze was blowing and an inch of new-fallen snow blanketed the center courtyard. The crypt-like Pentagon seeming more like its neighbor Arlington Cemetery than the beehive it was on any working day. I had read about the place, about the 25,000 people who worked here, but after 9 p.m., almost all the Pentagonians were at home. A strange, translucent barrier rose from the edge of the courtyard, ending in a slightly shimmering dome shape, within which, apparently, a spectacle would play out. It was obvious to us that neither interference — nor rescue — would be allowed. "You're prepared to sing to us?" Soreidian said, in a voice of highest ceremony. We stood before not eight but *eighteen* Lizardanians, ten of whom were new to us.

"You're asking us or telling us?" responded Brian in *Universalian*.

"Asking. Only asking," was the amused response. "Here is the place of war, isn't that it?" said Soreidian. "Tell us that humanity should be preserved before other races facing similar destruction. Let my people from your music frankly judge, as I believe they will, that you have nothing for us and that there is nothing we should do for you," Soreidian said the words loudly and with ceremony. He advanced to the judges, and to them he waved a great, clawed hand on which his fingers bore several large multicolored rings. His long cloak, yellow, orange and red, seemed to alternate between those shades, changing with and seeming to complement his strides. Brian and I wondered if our garments would similarly alter shades as we moved. The pattern changes were hypnotizing.

The words were foreign to the civilians and military service members still at the Pentagon. They stood on the cement steps and in the outdoor alcoves of the courtyard. They stared, mesmerized by the bizarre sight, utterly fascinated. I'm sure many only believed what they saw because it seemed like others believed. Foreign words, all — yet perfectly understandable to every listener.

Though the mesh of the costume, I could see Brian clearly. I could also see the scene before me in dazzling clarity, as though nothing covered my face at all.

Let's engage them, thought I to Brian.

Musical instruments arrived, floating down to the courtyard from the hovering Lizardanian ships. There very large piano and two guitars, which actually looked more like four guitars, two joined together. Brian was drawn to the smaller of the guitar-like instruments; I instantly seized the larger. There were straps on them, and we slid these over their shoulders, as naturally as putting on jackets or backpacks for school. My knowledge of music filled Brian's mind and words, and other music, very ancient, came to us both without effort.

Singing was the right choice...

I know you're right, but I usually only sing to myself, thought Brian.

Well, it's good you've been practicing because this time it counts.

And we sang. Our first song was in *Universalian.* Lizardania's language was just making itself

understood in our minds, *Universalian* came much
easier to us. Words from our song translated into
each listener's mind differently, but the emotion
sounded like this —

You've set our Moon in motion...
    We're met, each raised by the stars
    Crashing, cold oceans burning in our blood
    We know about our crimes and errors
    New to each other, a million miles from love
    Your silent ships, whirling over this cradle of hate
    Above our sadness and our many fears that it's
        already too late
    Soon you'll see we're not so different, that we all
     have doubt
    And we'll tell you, like it or not, what this pained
     Earth's truly about

You've set our World in motion...
    And for this moment, we've brewed powerful
     potions
    You've set our lives on dangerous missions
    It's ours to change Lizardania's notions and her
     baseless positions...
    We've just scratched the surface, tearing at old
     grounds
    Our dead next door, Sexton making his midnight
     rounds
    The night around us holds our secrets, (Everyone
     on guard!)
    Passages you've made too small, your hearts too
     hard

    Our people too primitive?
    Our saving song we feel might annoy

Forgive it, and know, by Neptune and Nature,
Twins you will allow to destroy

You've set our Hearts in motion...
Barometers of composure start to fall
A moment like this makes cowards of us all

You've set our Presentation in motion...
Took us each from the cold, lonely and crowded high
school hall
It's time to tell you, each and all
Well, we both know you!
Where planets and comets collide
We, both of us, made from the same Inspiration
A concept you cannot yet abide
(But you will, if not 'til later!)
It's time for us to SHOW (show) and TELL — we've
figured out the score

You've set our Stars in motion...
In this song you'll find not just self-serving promotion!
It's a humble request
Just us demanding to live, reap one more
harvest — (one more!)
Greater than hearts of youth will break
When you slam this final door

You've set our Defenses in motion...
Met here in our place of more-hate and less-love
We might yet fit like any hand in any glove
Let us make amends — and plans

You've set our Spirits in motion...
And kindled our deepest emotion!

We sang and we played, a kind of rock music of the stars, with classical and pop music mixed together, and we watched the Lizardanians who stood in judgment before us. When we ended this opening tune, which consumed somehow well over an hour, we were crestfallen as the Lizardanians turn their backs upon us.

Against us with the same language but a different tone, a deeper one, was music delivered by Danillia and Soreidian. It was devastating music. We sang a tale of hope for the good in humanity. The Lizardanians used the facts as they knew them and told their people to avoid the delusions of impracticality, to see things as they really were. They played their instruments and we played ours, only a few feet away. But it was not a cacophony of differing sounds. Rather one side, then the other, attempted to take over the music and direct it down opposite roads. The hearers could see both roads through our words, the notes and the tones. Which side would lose would depend on who had the right to choose — only the Lizardanian judges.

The time passed, and our fingers flew over the keys and the strings. I can do no justice to *Universalian* for you even now, but some thought they heard in our next music more than a little desperation. And I suppose they were right. Very roughly it was something like this:

We've sacrificed our wings
Thrown them out through the stars
If we've tossed away any glory
Well, this cost has always been ours

If our moment's past
If our fight's over before it's begun
Understand we felt a river crashed over us
With sword we stood before this outcast from the
 sun
Our victory you may deny,
Visions of togetherness you can decry

Is this sword too heavy?
And this day too long?
We'll fight on anyway
There's none right enough to call us wrong

Does love remain?
Guardian, I ask, even through Gia's final pain?

Everything is lost?
You won't help us pay this heavy cost?
Then we stand on summits cold,
Against the Twins only a few weeks old
Baby cries to the Heavens above,
Two stand between her, glove-in-glove

Out into the War Place,
Out of the school yard
You say we wait only for the world's applause?
That no one will believe in our lost cause?
If we be rebels without hope of tomorrow
Guardian! You really think we fear to beg, steal or
 borrow?
Well, you've taken no measure of our sorrow

Does love remain?
Even through the last hours of angel Gia's pain?

We're not all alone
There's still strength in these voices
We're not all alone
There's time and freedom left for right choices
Don't slam this door on us
It's not our last hour, that please trust
We've got the proof

You've heard it all before?
You insist to close this door?
Enough of our demands?
You won't let this witness take the stand?
Well, Guardian, you'll care what we say
By Draco's promise and the end of this long day.

But…Guardian, does love yet remain?

My fingers danced along the strings of the strange Lizardanian instrument. With a ferocious abandon, I played. I also played the piano they brought, it was like a synthesizer, but it was far more. Never before had I worked so hard at music, and I taught Brian as we went. He was a fast learner and supported what ended up being mostly my compositions with mostly his voice. We stole like thieves in the night every listener's imagination. Unskilled in musical instruments himself, Brian's knowledge of how to play the base guitar, the simplest of our choices, came nearly effortlessly. Brian surrendered his whole soul into the music, a song which captivated, but the strong faces of the Lizardanians gave no hint of favoring us.

Our in our second song, which somehow lasted 20 minutes longer than the first song, went on to describe our understanding of civilization.

In the meantime, a huge crowd gathered outside the Pentagon and atop its roof, the sky was full of helicopters and aircraft—mostly military people, which didn't help our case. It was as though they were waiting for orders.

While singing, we stayed rooted in the dusting of snow, surrounded by the high walls of the old, gray military building. Compared to Vermont, the snow here was only decorative. The walls shook and echoed with a tune which shamed the skill of countless military bands that had come before. I knew we were that good. Still, we had lost twice, the backs of the Lizardanians solemnly turned upon us. "Looks like everyone's interested in us—but, you know…we're not winning," whispered Brian. "I hope they can't see us like I can see you."

"And we're losing for everyone—for everything—in the world."

"It's too much responsibility," said Brian, looking at the bass-like guitar in his gloved hands. There were dozens of strings and various devices for changing tone and pitch. It was a device of divine and absolute perfection, the color an emerald green and, at the edges, Van Dike brown. I looked at my own instrument, cerulean blue, mostly, and a few colors that I just can't describe in English words. Neither of us felt we could tap their real potential. But the instruments seemed responsive to our every move, supportive of every note we played.

No fairy tale escaped either of us as children, and with our combined knowledge, we found the recurrent theme of love in countless mental images of books—*love* being the key to all things. But "right," "good," and even "love" didn't seem enough to convince the aliens to help. Nor did those qualities

seem to have a place here at the Pentagon. It seemed
to us, by clever design.

"You've closed your minds to our music," said
Brian boldly, realizing the end of the opening session
was approaching. He was tired already, but not too
tired to continue. "Because of your fear you avoid
coming to know us as more than just people who
need you. You'll learn that you're going to need us,
too!" That comment caused commotion among the
Lizardanian judges.

"Then we will hear you again tonight," said
Ettoros, speaking to us for the first time. He regarded
us with disdain and walked out of the company of the
judges.

"This fortress is responsible for war and the
deaths of millions of your race," said the Lizardanian,
looking squarely at Brian. "Why should we save your
people when you choose to destroy them
yourselves?"

I knew that Brian just hoped to run down the
clock for the day. His desire was anticipated.

The final exchange that evening was interrupted
by the arrival of the polygonal craft that had brought
us to the Pentagon. Brian and I could see that nothing
else could be accomplished with our first session. We
put our instruments reluctantly on the ground before
departing. It was like laying down our weapons in
defeat. Soldiers around the roof top of the Pentagon
were now visible; the gray light of dawn was
breaking. They held their weapons at the ready.
Thank the stars no one shot at the Lizardanians.
Human weapons would have had no effect on them,
we learned later. But they could have had an effect

on us, and there was no promise of defending us from our own people.

Just before we left, Brian decided to do something stupid (yes, I said *stupid*!). Brian looked over at Soreidian. The Lizardanian appeared completely on top to his game, invincible, not the least bit tired or worried. The creature looked down his long, equine face, cape pulled closely around him, in an apparent victory stance. That really burned Brian's butt, so he decided to tempt the killer instinct in the creature before him, projecting this thought—

I hate you for what you're doing – to my people – and I know you'll be paid out for this crime – soon, too!

It proved to be an unfortunate mental remark. Brian felt his mind snapped back by the biting and instant reply:

And I hate you, Brian Miller, for playing God and attempting to ruin my world to save your own! And you call THAT music? You will never master it before you are too tired. Why should your problems become ours? Your race is selfish, small minded and undeveloped, indifferent and hateful. It deserves this fate and I won't be 'paid out' for anything I do to you!

And as quickly, we were dropped off again in Vermont, without a word of farewell.

III

We walked down Har'dack Hill, the entire world changed. Forever. Our garments and headgear were safely hidden at the base of a maple tree on Har'dack Hill, covered over with pine branches.

"Damn it," whispered Brian, looking at the sun coming up over the hill to the east.

"Please don't swear, I've asked before," said I, absently.

"Okay. You're really worried that we won't find the way to win in time," he observed.

"I perform less well when I haven't rested," I admitted.

"Think there'll be school today?"

"If I were President, or whatever, I'd try to go for situation-normal. Yeah, I'd encourage everybody to go to work, to go to school, and let this thing play out on its own. If people don't want to keep society running today, what will make them do it tomorrow? They did that during 9/11, right? We can't afford to have everyone stop what they're doing, can we? I'm thinking we're seen aliens so much on TV that it's pretty much no big deal," said Brian, stepping out onto Congress Street from the woods. Right across was Smith Street.

At that instant, a car drove into view, coming over the crest of the hill. Realizing we mustn't be seen coming out of the woods at six in the morning, I dove into Brian, landing on top of him, behind a snow bank. The car passed by without stopping. Brian looked up at me. I could tell, just with the mental paths we'd made between us already, that he was wondering at the greenness of my eyes. For some reason, I didn't feel like getting off him right away. I just looked down at my trapped partner, there in the snow. His music was beautiful, his voice the same. If it was my fate to bear this burden, could I have found a better partner to suffer it with me? His heart was pure—but that wasn't enough! Strength wasn't and neither was intelligence, ability, love, charity, mercy, sacrifice — nothing was enough to compel the help Earth needed. What would work, how could this be done? Brian's smile dissolved as his thoughts went from me to the charge we shared. I bent down and I kissed him. He returned the pressure against my mouth and my warm breath returned some color to his pale cheeks.

CHAPTER SIX
School Lessons Aren't Enough

The world's leaders urged calm. It's what I would have done, that's for sure. Katrina wasn't as certain but she's not the chump I am. The President came on early morning television and told everyone to stay cool, but that wasn't necessary. The world held its breath—but then decided that moving on was better than standing still. Even so, a planet's worried opinions flooded forth and everyone was talking about the music we made at the Pentagon. The Web rocked with the recorded sounds of our music. Everyone understood what we were singing about, even if no one understood the words. I just hoped no one would put *us* and our music together...

Narrative Taken Over By Katrina's Father

Since neither Katrina nor Brian were present as we searched to learn their identities, nor later when I was at the White House, Katrina asked me to write about my meetings with our leaders. We were all worried, of course, but we Russians were certainly calmer than the Americans. I had no idea that my Katrina could be one of the singers. My suspicions came much later. In retrospect, I should have guessed.

"This is somewhat upsetting," said my superior officer, General Ivan Krahotkin, exercising his powers of understatement. I sat at a large conference table, in a very secretive and secure section of the American's Defense Intelligence Agency at Ft. Meade, Maryland.

"I mean, your intelligence service coming to ours like this. I suppose for people like me who can recall our former relationship so vividly — well, it would be humorous if the situation were less...*unpleasant,* shall we say?" General Krahotkin is perhaps our best general in Russia.

"This is the most serious situation in history, anywhere!" blurted out General Frank Atwood, rising to his feet from the American side of the table. The Americans don't generally like our stoic view of the world.

"Our civilian leadership is at its wits' end and has turned this into a purely military operation," General Atwood told us. He was the Chairman of the Joint Chiefs of Staff, America's top general. "We want to make it a *joint military operation,* it's the only hope, the only way." He regained some control and reseating himself. We deputies on both sides shifted uneasily.

"We have two people just waltz into the frickin' Pentagon and start singing?! And now everyone knows that there are asteroids coming to wipe out the planet — that's plain. So American intelligence wants to find out who in the hell these two people are!" barked General Atwood.

"You think we have something to do with all this — do I understand your position correctly?" General Yegor Ilyitch Yahzov's heavy accent pushed out his English like a Russian icebreaker. He was the deputy to General Krahotkin.

"You have us right."

"It's just lucky for you that you beat us economically — I'd have loved to hear you struggling with Russian rather than me struggling with English," said Yahzov. At first there was silence. Then there was some needed laughter — much ice was now cracked if not broken. Outside, the winter's evening had deposited a half inch of snow, encouraging many Washingtonians to take the day off, despite what the American President had said that morning about ignoring last night's bizarre events. I thought about the disaster it would be if Russians in Moscow took the day off because of snow.

"Regardless of how things turned out over a decade ago, we need your help in finding these people, and soon — who knows what's coming next?" General Atwood was insistent. "And if we can't get your help, we'll go it alone," he added.

General Krahotkin sighed.

I had been called back from Montreal to discuss the strange case. I also knew there was some suspicion about me personally.

"We'll do all we can to identify these people and share the information with you," I said calmly.

"Thank you — now, Colonel Chakiaya, you just arrived at your station in Canada, isn't that right?" Yahzov asked me.

"That wasn't you last night at the Pentagon, was it?" General Atwood cut in. He walked, and often strayed over, the line between bluntness and rudeness.

"No."

"Uh, Colonel Chakiaya has his family with him, a daughter, a son, his wife. Also a professional colleague has just arrived," offered General Krahotkin.

"Do I understand that there was a, ah, *spacecraft* spotted in Moscow not long before your departure for Canada? It fit the description — geez, it's amazing to be talking like this — matched the description of one of those seen over the Pentagon?" General Atwood finished as best he could, chuckling just a little, without much mirth behind it.

"We have that information, yes," I told him.

"But you don't know anything else? Or that another of these damn alien ships was seen within a hundred miles of your new location?"

"If I did, I'd tell you and, of course, my superiors in this very room," I tried to check my temper. I felt time was being wasted. The identity of the shrouded figures held no particular intrigue for me. Had I guessed one was my own daughter, I wonder if I could have hidden the knowledge. Silence ruled for several painful seconds.

"We want to assign some agents to accompany you back to Montreal. There is some connection here and I'm sure with your help, we'll find it," said General Atwood. He still regarded me with suspicion. There were lots of facts, but no obvious connection between them. The stars on his shoulder boards gleamed at me, along with his penetrating, suspicious eyes.

"Could you please get on your feet, Colonel Chakiaya?" said General Atwood.

"Excuse us?" surprise was General Krahotkin's master.

"Please just have him *get the hell up* — your English is good enough for that, but I guess you don't need reminding that we don't know the appropriate Russian words," General Atwood answered stiffly. "I thought we wouldn't need a translator for this session. Damn it, go find me one," he added to an aid.

"Rudeness isn't necessary, not at a time like this," I finally told him.

"*Spaciba*," said the American general shortly, trying to use the word for "please." Clearly it was never his favorite word, in any language. "Could you just stand up, okay?"

That made me smile. I stood.

Two soldiers appeared on either side of me. A tape measure was produced. The soldiers measured my height quickly without touching my uniform, one scribbled a number on a piece of paper. The paper was as quickly handed to General Atwood.

"They're shorter than you," said the general. "Okay, you can sit down."

"Who?"

"These two negotiators."

"Is that what we're calling them now?"

"That's what I'm calling them now. I'm not speaking for the U.S. Government, just myself. Obviously something is being bargained for, and its got to do with those asteroids. It's being done through music, this operatic rock music, or whatever it is. I admit I like it, but catchy tunes aren't in my department. I'd never have thought it would end quite like this — who would? No one understands the words, but we all understood the meaning, for the most part. The voices are being analyzed now but our people can't reach any conclusions. The intonation and parlance of this singing is remarkably different from any human language. But we can't even be sure that the shrouded figures are human at all…who knows, time will tell. Hell, I don't know. It wasn't supposed to end like this for me," General Atwood said helplessly, and shook his shaved head and looked down at this briefing papers. He was a simple person, and he was faced with something complicated. I could almost forgive his frustration. I had the luxury of not being in charge. Staring at his clasped fingers on the table before him, gazing at his West Point ring, he added, "and we've got to figure out who these people are, if they are humans."

"Why?"

"Ivan Semyonovich, for a scientist, quite a bit needs to be explained to you," interjected General Krahotkin in a warning tone. Orders from the top were to avoid antagonizing the Americans.

The American general stood. "You're free to leave for Montreal, Colonel Chakiaya. We'll let you know if we need anything else. Don't be alarmed if some people introduce themselves to you soon. There will be a lot of interest in your neck of the woods if those ships have their trajectories traced back to Canada. Expect to be back in Washington on short notice…ah, *please*."

"It's my opinion that we should let this singing or these meetings or whatever they are continue without our interference. We could be undoing our salvation," I ventured.

"Or we could be interfering with a planned alien invasion of this planet," snorted General Atwood.

" — that makes the least sense to anyone here? Don't we have two huge asteroids heading right for us — the Near Earth Object studies have predicted this event—who'd want to invade us with planetary destruction a certainty?" I asked in an outraged tone, finally stepping over the edge. I wish my wife could have explained things, she is more diplomatic than I am, actually.

"That will do, Colonel Chakiaya!" said General Krahotkin, though he secretly agreed with my every word, as he told me later.

I was leaving when I heard over my shoulder,

"It's got something to do with that man, that man right there, you should arrest that guy," said the General Atwood, regarding his Russian counterpart.

As I picked up my brief case and winter coat and gloves I heard Krahotkin respond.

"Our best people are working on this, General. We can...cooperate, yes? We're sending Avilov, Preobrazhensky and Kropotkin—agents well known to your intelligence services, per our very old understanding in such matters."

The last thing I heard before leaving was General Atwood saying, "Our people are ready to share all we have with them. We have agents in Montreal already. We'll find these two, they have to be stopped, and quick—*by any means necessary.*"

II

"Did you hear that the American president is speaking again soon?" Katrina asked me. She said it as she came to meet me for our walk to school.

"Yup. And we have a school day, as predicted!" I couldn't help saying.

We walked through two inches of new snow covering the eight inches already down. Cars struggled along in the road as we walked down Fairfield.

"My Uncle Vanya gets Russian stations. There were a lot of high level meetings. The military is on alert. I tried to call my father but only Mama was there. Seems strange. She said Papa was out of town."

"They suspect you," I told her. "Or they will soon, I can feel it."

"Oh, no, certainly not," Katrina was dismissive. "How could they know?"

"Maybe they don't yet, but they will, they'll put it together. Besides, it's something that Torrillian said that makes me think like that. Remember how he said they might get us and that we must fail? "He said we must *fall*, not *fail*. Falling sounded worse, coming from him. My mind is racing, I'm learning so much. Brian, I'm learning ancient arts of healing and other things, all about our galaxy — the galaxy is alive and vital, not cold, empty and remote. I just knew it!"

"Not Ms. Starblue again," I sighed as the bell rang. We were standing under it, and the metal echoed when it stopped, the way those old bells do. Katrina reached out, took my hand and rested her cheek against it.

"I know we can do it, Brian. We'll figure it out because we just have to!"

"Okay, this hour's ours — we know what she wants to do, so lets take it to her first," said I, rewarding my friend with the passion she needed to see just then. "We know our own people in that room better than she does, and we have to challenge her assumptions and jump on her crap right off. I think it's a tribute to our race that we're just going to work, going to school, and living our lives even with disaster up in our faces — that has to impress them...*positively!*"

Katrina looked down with the task of table-turning.

"I agree," she said, actually stomping her foot! "Let me lead off — 'crap' isn't a bad word, right?" She seemed rejuvenated.

We went boldly into class, and stopped short at the door.

Mr. Brodsky, the principal, was talking quietly with Ms. Starblue. A lesson plan was between them on the long, skinny conference table next to the teacher's desk. Other students shuffled in.

"Class," Mr. Brodsky got everyone's attention immediately, "We all know about the extraordinary events taking place right now. We also know that the president has asked for calm and, as far as I know, generally gotten it. He wants us to continue in our daily routines and lives and trust in those assigned to this challenge to handle it. I for one am going to do so. As principal of this school, I plan to continue my daily effort in that job — and I want you to continue doing your job as students. It's a strange time, but I know we'll get through this. This school, and this world, is a good place as long as you and I make it so — and you're in the right place. So today I'm observing our new student teacher, Ms. Starblue because Ms. Blodgett has called in sick," Mr. Brodsky's opening was immediately leapt on by Ms. Starblue who seemed very fresh and rested.

"Well another new person, Mr. Brodsky, is Ms. Chakiaya and she has certainly had an ample share of my instruction, haven't you dear? Perhaps, because you're new in this country, you can tell Mr. Brodsky what time with me has been like, so he can know what he's in for," she grinned and was apparently thinking many moves ahead, preparing her next attacks, like some superhuman chess computer. I couldn't believe how brash she was being. But to look at the little woman, you'd never have known what she really was.

You don't have to expend yourself on her, Kat, she wants to wear you down and make you fight where and when it doesn't count. Save yourself, save your energy, save your answers for tonight when it means something. Rest your mind if you can! I thought the words desperately but soothingly toward my friend. I could see Katrina's fists under the desk, her face flushing with anger. Had Katrina a pencil in her hand, I felt certain it would have been turned to dust.

"I think," said Katrina, "that Ms. Starblue's instruction, Mr. Brodsky, is why people like her enjoy the reputation they have today."

The puzzling reply caught everyone off guard, to include Ms. Starblue. She was obviously was having a very difficult time translating the words in her mind.

Ms. Starblue knew Katrina and I were feeding off each other, getting words, concepts, phrases not only from our mutual stockpile of knowledge but from the vast database of Lizardanian knowledge. That we humans were permitted to randomly wade around in Lizardania's shoreless seas of ancient learning was more than Ms. Starblue could stand. She felt positively violated at the thought.

"Thank you for joining us today, Mr. Brodsky, and yes, we're living through interesting times," Ms. Starblue smiled sweetly, attempting to ignore my friend, which she couldn't. But then Ms. Starblue looked at me.

"I thought given the bizarre events of last night," she went on, "since no one is thinking about much else, that we might try to figure out what we saw going on with those Lizardanians. Some of you look really tired, too, it must be that many of us stayed up all night watching the television too long. Brian, you look like one of these and so do some others of you — I can only recommend that you get your sleep and not worry about those things that are naturally occurring and outside our ability to change," intoned Ms. Starblue. "But first we have to get through some of our algebraic homework — perhaps Mr. Miller will do our first few problems *up at the board.*"

I wanted to swear real bad, almost as much as I wanted to get stoned. But I slashed both feelings away with a mental sword thrust.

Kat, she just wants you and I to waste energy on fighting with her. We don't need that. Mr. Brodsky will notice any attacks and ask her about it. I think we should just go along with it.

Yeah, I see that now myself.

But we reckoned without the Lizardanian who wouldn't be denied. Before she could repeat her ordering me to the chalk board, someone spoke up in a sarcastic voice.

"Howd'ya know what they're called, there, Ms. Starblue?" the interruption momentarily derailed Danillia's plans to wear me down.

It was Justin Mack, still sore about the "lesson" that Ms. Starblue intended to teach him.

"Hmmm?" The student teacher turned innocently from the algebraic formulas she was scratching into the blackboard for me to work. The problems were hopelessly complex. I felt Katrina remembering that she would have to deal with the

83

math and science part of our debate, and that would be facing us during the Presenting, sooner than later — probably tonight. Those were Ms. Starblue's departments. But she was going after me now to keep Katrina helping me and spending energy. Mr. Triassic would stay on history and political and social issues with me. Together they'd exhaust us both — and soon.

"I said, how do you know that those lizard things are called 'Lizardanians'?" Justin's suspicions were primitive, the guy's such a cro-mag. He was just trying to give Ms. Starblue a hard way to go. If he'd only known...if he's only known....

She smiled sweetly at Justin and the class.

"Well, Justin, that's because...*I am a Lizardanian myself*, isn't that right, Brian Miller?"

"Yeah, right," I said automatically. "And not the nicest one I've met, either."

Katrina was thunderstruck and looked warily around the room. For a moment, no one said anything.

But then Mr. Brodsky started laughing before anyone else did and then the room of students joined in, the place shaking with hilarity. The student teacher only blushed and smiled meekly. She glanced at me and Katrina, swaying back and forth like a schoolgirl on one heel, innocently waiting for the laughter to die down. When it did, Not-Ms. Starblue walked back to the blackboard from where she'd wandered during her exchange with Justin.

"Alright, now, everybody stop that laughing, geezum crow!" said she, "this isn't really a joking situation."

Mr. Brodsky grinned widely at the faux-teacher's wit. Katrina sucked her teeth loudly. Ms. Starblue's thievery of a favorite Vermont expression really made me wretch.

"Not for us, anyway," said Ms. Starblue, winking openly at me. "Now let's take a look at these lovely problems, there's something that will apply to our basic algebra, something that our little negotiators — or whatever they're styling themselves to be — might profit by learning…even little I can see that! Brian, come on up and show us some of the answers!"

Ms. Starblue then turned her back — a little too quickly — to the class. Katrina and I fumed, realizing the quick turn of the back was meant to remind us of last night's losses.

The class went rapidly along, with Ms. Starblue making her speculations about the strange events as we went through the math lesson. She kept me at the board, doing out one problem after the next, taxing both me and Katrina. The Russian's native competitive streak kept her spending mental energy on feeding me the right answers — but there were no Lizardanian judges in the classroom to give us credit. The mathematical relations were made clear to all, but she kept me up at the board a long, long time, Katrina mentally coaching me.

Finally the bell rang, and I felt like a prize fighter ready to limp back to my corner. My brain felt like it was on fire. As we left, we saw Mr. Brodsky walk up to the front. He and Ms. Starblue began talking quietly.

"What do you mean they won't lie?" Katrina asked me, coming up to my locker. A group of girls were talking about me a couple of doors down.

"I see you remain popular despite your troubles," observed Katrina with just the slightest hint of jealously in her tone. I really like that.

"Yeah, it's like…kinda inexplicable…you know, *scandaluze*," I told her, trying to make her laugh.

"Scandalous? That's something we're trying to avoid," was her serious reply. Touchy!

Evening arrived quickly, the sky in our part of Vermont cloudless, the day done, and our grim judges meeting us in silence on Har'dack Hill precisely at 9:00 p.m.

CHAPTER SEVEN
Cars in Black

Evening went terribly.

Everyone watching, on or off-world, witnessed a thorough beating for Brian and for me. Again, our Presentation garments were stashed on Har'dack Hill. The urge to sleep was nearly too great to resist. The lead weight of failure was heavier than the burden of sleeplessness and hunger when we crunched through the deep snow and off Har'dack Hill, back in our school clothes. Dawn broke mercilessly. I couldn't recall being so tired.

We walked straight into Brian's house, like zombies, not even able to care if we were seen on the road at that hour. Breakfast would consist of nothing but Lizardanian water.

Our singing could not have been better, but at the end of each musical movement, the backs of the Lizardanians were solemnly turned on us — and our world. It was beyond failing a test, having one's lunch money stolen, getting a nasty pimple before a big date...it was...the worst of all failings because we were failing for everyone and everything, not just ourselves.

Soreidian and Danillia were constantly hitting us with the unexpected, to include a terrible location — a garbage heap in the Philippines! The gut-wrenching stench was almost as overpowering as the initial vision of the site itself. I couldn't believe we'd be made to fight — to sing — from such a place. It was hopeless. The session inflicted maximum possible damage to our cause, but we fought the best we could to make humanity's case for salvation. I did brilliant work with the mathematical and physics challenges set before me by Danillia, all on a giant, semi-transparent blackboard. Those challenges were between song sets, as our operatic rock music ripped through the long night — but it was only night in Vermont. The sun was out during much of our music. The sight of the Lizardanian judges, in their beautiful robes, standing there in the trash mounds, was so embarrassing to me that at first I could sing nothing. How many other such places were there in a world teaming with overpopulation and polarized wealth for the few, hunger the lot of the many? How could we excuse such places? And where would they pick next? I could think of even worse places, perhaps a prison in a backward country, or a poorly run mental institution…and I shuttered.

Personal defeat we could take. But failing for humanity? For all the world's innocent little creatures and lovely living things? It was beyond our ability to endure. It all but broke me, that awful night. We actually rallied and fought back toward the end of the Presentation, our music on key, instruments precisely in tune. But to no avail. Some of the Lizardanians were moved by the music, even as they stood among the smelly trash piles. But we still couldn't get most of the Lizardanians not to turn their backs — three, though, continued to face us during our final two songs. It seemed too little a victory, far too late. The loudness of our music still echoed in our ears.

Tonight more than just Lizardanians would be in attendance, we were told before leaving the steamy Philippines to arrive back in frozen Vermont. Another day gone.

The morning news was on. We watched impassively in Brian's kitchen. Nothing was discussed in any depth except the twin comets approaching the planet and the strange musical warfare that lasted for hours, until daylight, *Eastern Standard Time*, a reporter noted. If the media had noticed the clue, the intelligence services would also. Why were the debates always at the same time? Many minds were at work trying to figure out who and where we were. They were getting nearer.

"Company for breakfast today, Brian?"

I was so far down the road to total exhaustion that I didn't immediately notice Brian's mother entering the kitchen.

"I tried to wake you up last night to watch the news with me, but you wouldn't come down..." said she to my friend with a suspicious pitch to her voice. "Hello. Uh, you'd be Brian's friend, right? You're here for breakfast too?"

We said nothing.

"So I went up to get you out of bed," went on Brian's mother, busying about the kitchen. "And you weren't there, Brian."

Brian looked up from his water glass.

"Sorry Mom," was all he said.

"Brian said it would be okay to have breakfast

over here, Ms. Miller," I managed, trying to be calm
and change the subject.

"There were some strange cars parked across the
street last night, Brian," said his mother, servicing the
breakfast table. She eyed us carefully, noticed that we
just moved our spoons around the cereal with longing
looks. Normally we'd both be gobbling the stuff
down. She noticed I ate nothing.

"Cars, it seems to me, can't be strange, ma'am.
But there are strange people in cars, sometimes," my
helpless observation wasn't helping. I just looked
down at my bowl, stirring the cereal as if looking for a
lost ring in the flakes. Or maybe just for a way to
win—but nothing hopeful came to the surface.

"Dark cars and the men in them had dark suits
and dark glasses," said Ms. Miller. "They left only
about an hour ago."

"Oh."

"So how were the dumb singing debates or
whatever, Ms. Miller," asked I, immediately
regretting it. I took toast over to my of the table,
buttered it slowly, but didn't eat.

"Well, I guess you didn't have time to watch what
the whole world are watching every night—any more
than Brian," now Ms. Miller sounded very suspicious.
"It's more popular than American Idol."

She looked at us. We turned our tired eyes away.
Ms. Miller probably at first presumed we were out
last night on a secret date…but then something else
occurred to her.

Her coffee cup fell from her hands, shattering on
the floor.

"My God, it's you two, isn't it?" she whispered.

"Let's go Brian, 'might as well be early," said I to
him, sliding off my chair and heading to the door.

"Right."

"Kids, listen—" began Ms. Miller, moving to get in front of us.

"Mom, *you'll* have to listen on this one," said Brian, turning on her and grabbing her forearm. "The Earth depends on our finishing what we've started. Even if we can't win, we're still the only chance—"

Ms. Miller's tears burst forth. "—It's so unfair...why!" And the woman turned on me, as if it were all my doing.

"Why does it have to be my Brian—why him?" She pulled him to her and would not let him go. I came up to the weeping mother, gently touching her shoulder. How long would it be before my uncle figured it out, or my own parents?

"Because I'm here, Moms...me and Kat...and nobody else. Just us. Katrina and I are between the way things ought to be and the way that it is. It's a tough place to be, Mom. Katrina and I just have to deal with this. Please don't stop us. Don't let *them* stop us. It's about...life itself now. Can you see that, Moms?"

Ms. Miller cupped Brian's face and gently up toward her own. She was a tall woman, but he was almost level with her, though not quite. I stood by in silence.

"Okay," said Brian's mother, mastering herself. "Okay, Brian...all right. No one gets it out of me—but why, why does it have to be you two?"

"I don't know, Moms, I bet there are a million kids, a billion, better suited than me to do this thing—without Kat, I wouldn't know the first thing about singing or playing the instruments we've been given. But this work is ours to do, for some reason. So we're going to do it," Brian's resolution brought a smile to his mother.

"You let them know if they hurt either of you, then…then…well, they'll answer to me," she said.

"Sure, Moms. Don't worry, we can handle 'em."

I had to give Brian a sidelong long and my signature smirk.

Ms. Miller watched us go from the porch. I bet she scarcely noticed the cold.

We walked slowly to school.

I was thinking about saying something encouraging to him…but then I noticed something.

"We're being followed."

Brian casually shoved his gloved hands in his blue jean pockets and got a very stolid, almost a Russian look of resignation to fate. Then he looked over to where I nodded. A sloppily-dressed 40-something male was paralleling us on the opposite side of Fairfield Street. The man had a long, tattered black overcoat.

"And watched — there's another one," Brian nodded slightly up the street. A woman sat in an idling car reading the town newspaper, *The Messenger*. She looked very briefly toward us, then went back to her paper.

"Should we even go back into the school?" I wondered.

"I'm betting the Lizardanians want to play this thing out as much as we do. Maybe they want to send a signal throughout the galaxy that they make no special exceptions in their stupid policy of not helping people in trouble. I think they'll protect us once we're in the building just like Ms. Starblue saved me from Justin and his buddies."

"Or," my friend countered, "they'll let these people capture us, and rid themselves of any obligation to continue the singing, simply because our race was primitive and self-destructive and ruined their own chances to avoid the Twins by arresting their only representatives."

He looked over at me and grinned in his mischievous way.

"Like that about *sucks*! I like my prediction a lot better--you Russians are about morbid, *geezum crow*!" said Brian with a nervous laugh.

"You're a dreamer,"

"You wanna back out, say so. Just forget the whole thing?" said he.

"All this wasn't my idea. And there's no where to go, you know that."

"I was kidding, ohmuhgod" and he added seriously, "I know what has to be done."

The school was just ahead, we were within shouting distance of our schoolmates.

"There's another one by the door — I think they've been watching too many old movies, this reading-the-paper-to-avoid-suspicion crap? That guy there is dressed like a food worker, and I'm picking him out from here. Look, he's scanning the crowd for us, what a dip," said Brian.

"So now your government's after us and we haven't exactly progressed in our work, have we? And 'crap' isn't a swear word, right? What about 'sucks'? — I'll find that in your mind, on my own. Brian...I feel my best music is behind me. I'm so tired that I...I can't *feel* my life. I know that sounds crazy."

"Try drugs; that's when you don't feel your life. But your music might have been more convincing than we know."

"Or less."

"Don't be a pessimist. It's just the end of the world, hey, no worries!" Brian teased.

II

Won't Lizardania help us Present tonight?

I thought it to Brian, nearing Social Studies, after he'd calmed down a little. I dreaded Ms. Starblue — she would be ready, completely fit, without a hint of wear or tare, waiting to rip us up, with those cleverly hidden mental claws.

I don't know.

We stood at the door to Social Studies. We entered and joined the other kids. As Brian sat down he glanced warily at Justin Mack and his sidekick Derek Peters. They'd been whispering the moment Brian and I came in, then they stopped.

My gangstas got something going down, thought Brian to me.

I've learned enough about Lizardanian fighting tactics to take care of all three, even though I'm tired, was my response. *Shall I?*

'Might attract unneeded attention, don't you think?

It matters anymore?

We'll see. It's not over yet, you look like you're still awake, and that's good...

I'm not awake by an awful lot.

Doesn't look like Ms. Starblue taught them enough, first time. It'd have been enough for me, I can tell you that.

We exchanged glances from across the aisle. We waited for Ms. Starblue. The Lizardanian's form of telepathy was overpowering. It wasn't what Brian or

I expected at all. It was like playing a music instrument, or typing or riding a bike.

Ms. Starblue was late, most unlike a Lizardanian.

Of a sudden, Ms. Starblue burst into class, causing everyone to jump. The door rebounded hard off the stopper on the wall.

"Well, this hour looks like it's completely mine again today," she said in her thick, Eastern European sounding voice, smirking at Brian and me. She went immediately to the teacher's closet with her overcoat in hand—she looked so eager to get at Brian and I.

Brian saw it long before I did.

A motorcycle engine was propped on top of the partly opened closet door, poised to fall. The engine must have been 90 pounds, at least. You couldn't see it because the projection screen was cleverly pulled down. Only someone from the far right of the class, as Brian was, would have noticed it.

It was so bizarre a sight that Brian was frozen. Obviously the Mack gang wanted payback for Ms. Starblue's earlier insult. Without thinking for an instant, Brian only saw someone in danger. It was just like him. He jumped forward and flashed a thought at me. Realizing on the instant, I was on my feet.

Brian and I later learned that tremendous energy when into maintaining the image of a human. It dulled the Lizardanian's awareness. Danillia was, though she didn't show it, wearied by the singing of the evenings before. She'd wanted a debate from the beginning, which would have drawn on her more developed skills and helped preserve her prodigious strength. As it was, she'd never thought her voice lovely, and now that was giving out, every bit as bad as mine. She was closer to exhaustion than Brian and

I guessed. The Lizardanian argument still held sway, they thanked the Galaxies, but would it tonight?

She did not look up at the engine teetering above, reaching out for the knob of the closet. She was still wondering why we weren't broken.

"Look out!" hollered Brian racing up the aisle.

"Brian!" But I was too far away to help.

Ms. Starblue was out of the way of the falling weight only because Brian threw himself into her. Brian's left shoulder was not completely clear as the engine came down with a loud, metallic crash. The engine had come from the next-door shop class. It was perched on the teacher's closet door with diabolical calculation, which is just like that pug-faced, yard ape, Justin.

I raced to Brian, and knelt on the floor beside him.

"Are you alright?!" I'd seen the engine hit him, but as yet there was no sign of blood, everyone wearing long sleeves on the cold winter day.

Ms. Starblue was on her feet with inhuman speed, poised for a fight. Cold assessment of what happened was completed in seconds — and she saw an opportunity. Both Ms. Starblue and I reached to haul Brian up.

Do you think I owe you rotten kids something for that! The voice was incredibly loud in our heads.

Do you think such toys can harm me! Why don't you brats just give up! You can't beat me, you can't win! How dare you attempt to curry favor with me over nothing, NOTHING! The creature seemed beside herself with rage. We wondered if she'd reveal herself. But outwardly she displayed only good humor. I detected just a tinge of guilt, too, when her last words penetrated our minds. Kids in class exchanged whispers and giggles.

I quickly guided Brian back into his seat and nearly threw him into it.

Why the HELL are you helping her after what she's done to us! After what you KNOW she'll let happen to the entire planet! What the HELL are you thinking, dumb ass! I was so furious at him that I even borrowed lightly from his extensive cuss collection.

All the women in my life are angry with me. And don't swear — it's beneath you! he thought playfully to me. I couldn't tell how badly he was hurt.

I recovered my own seat in a few moments, amid the undercurrent of snickering and whispers. The student teacher walked to the front of the classroom.

She was in trouble, I had to help, Brian thought to me, with a grimace masking his face.

She could probably crush that engine in one hand! If it fell off a bridge and hit her in the head it wouldn't have hurt her.

You don't EVEN know that.

I know how strong they are, and so should you by now.

But they're not invincible.

Oh, Brian — think! If you get yourself hurt, we're both done. How bad is it?

Not bad, really.

Liar.

I know my secret's safe with you!

"It seems that Mr. Miller had second thoughts about his little practical joke," said Ms. Starblue calmly to the perplexed students.

"Lucky for him," she winked at the class, tossed her head and laugh a little. "Mr. Mack, would you kindly go and inform Mr. Brodsky of Brian's little prank? We'll need a few volunteers to haul this into the hallway to restore it to the shop class. Isn't that where you got it, Mr. Miller?"

I was furious. I heard whispering from the class like "bussstteed!" and "auhhhh," and "suspension ciitttaaahhh".

What's she trying to do! I'm going to tell her off.

No, no, don't; don't take the bait. She knows better, best to think nothing to her, nothing. It'll be okay. I'll deny it obviously, Brodsky'll probably believe me.

I worried that Brian would be hauled off. Could things get worse? Oh, if I could just get that Justin, Dirk and Derek alone for five minutes...those morons would ruin what little chance there was! I'd turn the three of them into garden soil for everyone else's good.

In minutes a little knock at the door, and we had company.

"Please come in," said Ms. Starblue brightly.

Principal Brodsky walked in with three people — and Justin too, who took his seat with a grin aimed at Brian. "You're crucified..." he hissed as he passed Brian's desk. The newcomers were dressed very casually, almost nondescriptly.

"Can we help you...other people?" Ms. Starblue looked a little uncertain because she only expected the principal.

That one is Sergei Sosnovsky. He's in the Russian intelligence service! The others must be spies also. My dad pointed out Sosnovsky to me once in Moscow and said to stay away from him. I've never seen the other two.

For a moment, Brian didn't say anything.

I just thought this Sosnovsky's identity to Danillia and Soreidian, but I'm not sure if they heard me because they haven't thought anything back, Brian intimated to me moments later.

Say WHAT!?

Sorry — but if they haul me or you out of class where

*will we be? The Lizardanians have to be relied on to
protect us.*

*Brian, you're giving them way too much credit for fair
play – they might be glad to see us get arrested right here
and right now!*

The possibility hadn't crossed Brian's tired mind,
apparently.

"Ah, Ms. Starblue, Mr. Mack tells me you had
some, uh, engine trouble here recently?" the principal
sounded very much in control of the situation, as
though secret agents in class were entirely routine.
The room giggled – it was great entertainment and
got everyone's mind off the impending global
calamity and our regular work.

"It seems that Mr. Miller has been using his
popularity around the school to take advantage of
me," said the student teacher batting her long, utterly
phony lashes. I could have hurled right then.

"These gentlepersons asked to observe one of our
classes and I suggested yours – they're from a New
Hampshire college and have an interest in observing
our instruction of this particular group of students. I
suppose even in extraordinary times, we all have our
jobs to do."

Their group moved to the free desks at the back
of the room. They had clipboards, but they didn't
look interested in noting methods of instruction.

*It's like a little league parent volunteer going up
against a professional football team coach at the Super
Bowl. We've got toddlers up against 300 pound
linebackers.*

You really think it's that bad.

You're asking me or telling me?

Asking, silly, thought Katrina.

No.

Oh, good.
It's a whole helluva lot worse.
No, it's not. And don't swear; next time I'm smacking you.

Ms. Starblue launched into an attack on the motives of the Founding Fathers and their treatment of slaves and Native Americans. Brian and I were both too tired and to be drawn into her traps. Mr. Triassic would have his turn with us next hour, and so it would go all day long until that evening.

I knew that none of the agents had any intention of letting Brian or I leave the school at day's end.

CHAPTER EIGHT
Time, *Stand Still!*

Katrina and I met for the break between 2nd and 3rd hour in the basement male/female bathroom. When the bell rang, we boogied without looking back.

"'You doing okay?" I asked.

"Exhausted doesn't tell half the story. My concentration is going fast. I wish I could believe they were as weak. I swear they're invincible. Did you hear Soreidian say he could save us and our families? Damn it, Brian. Sometimes surrender is the only way. They'll save thirty of us, and our families...don't you think maybe we've had...enough?" She looked so tired. All the proud Russian fight seemed drained.

"Don't swear. You got me on that cussing thing. What an influence you are!" And I held her tight. "What happens to everyone — and everything — else?"

She took a deep breath. A moment of silence passed.

"No. I can't walk away...*of course I can't*," she let me go.

We heard something. Sound of the bathroom door opening. We stood very still.

"We're made," I whispered.

"Huh?"

"That means someone knows! Didn't find that one in my head yet, huh?"

"It's my people. They've come for me," Katrina said.

I swatted the door open with authority. There was nothing else to be done. The WHACK against the adjoining door sounded like a rifle shot. Before us were Justin, Derek and Dirk.

"Miller, you got this coming, maggot!" said Justin, stepping forward.

I

"Good afternoon, my fellow Americans. For the last few days we've all been captured by the images on our television screens of an extraordinary spectacle. I appreciate the way we have continued to do the work of the nation. People depend on people to be there for them, even in strange and extraordinary times like these. We've been watching a series of debates conducted in music between an alien race and, we believe, two of our own kind. It seems like science fiction brought into everyday life, but it's happening, and we accept that. I'm proud of the way we as a nation, and the world as a people, are dealing with it. In the midst of trying to interpret these events, we've learned from the National Aeronautical and Space Administration what has been corroborated by scientists in other nations. Two asteroids are speeding toward the Earth on a collision course. Their speed and composition are beyond our technology to combat or avoid. There is no reason to panic because there is no where to go and nothing we can do about it. I'm in close consultation with our friends and allies. The world's leaders are also in the process of addressing their own nations about the facts. We believe that the aliens debating whether or not to help us is based on what they are being told. Staying calm and continuing with our lives is, we believe, the best message we can send to these two brave young people representing us.

I know it's extraordinary, but there are the facts. As your President, I have always leveled with you and told you what I know about important events. To make the right impression, it makes cooperation and living in peace all the more important. We have to work together not just as a nation, but as a world. We are asking those two engaged in these conversations with these aliens to please come forward and talk to us about convincing the aliens to help us destroy the asteroids. While we appreciate why they might want to remain anonymous, we have to find them and try to learn how to avoid the consequences of a strike from the twin asteroids. We expect everyone to carry on their lives and activities and to remain strong within the embrace of their families, their religious faiths, and to reach out to those less fortunate. I know each of you want to help and in the days to come there may be much you can do. But until then, I'm asking for your patience and I'm asking you to carry on with your life, so that we can all carry on with our lives, as best we can. As soon as we know more, we'll inform you. Thank you for your support for the challenging days ahead and

God bless you, God Bless America, and may God bless our Earth."

II

Katrina and I were unavailable for the assembly called by Principal Brodsky. So we missed the President's message played in the large auditorium from live television. We were a little busy.

They must have followed us down! I thought to my friend.

Glad they've decided to let us get a little more up close and personal.

See that broom and mop behind Dirk?

Yes, I do.

Weapons — I don't like this any more than you do. But we don't have time for these losers. Let's see what that Lizardanian training can do.

I agree — but I didn't say I didn't like it.

"Okay, Miller! Out o' that stall, yah gob!" Justin sounded pissed. He was holding a pipe. The others were armed the same.

We unpacked ancient arts, like opening overstuffed suitcases, deadly techniques were being placed in the many-shelved dressers in our heads. Anything might be selected and then dished out.

One-Two-Three!

Though Dirk and Derek moved up, Katrina and I blew past them. She did an armless summersault and I a regular one, landing before the cleaning equipment. I'd never somersaulted in my life — now it seemed like second nature. Katrina had the broom; I had the mop. In synchronized motion, we each brought a foot down on the business end of our cleaning tools, snapping them into three foot long sections. We faced the three at what must have seemed very odd angles, standing almost sideways and nearly backward to the punks.

Justin, Dirk and Derek exchanged quizzical questions, laughing, and did not back away.

"Oh man, Miller! You and your Russian chick gonna hit us with some sticks?" The three thugs edged closer, their foot-long pipes raised menacingly.

"Time for a whoopin'! I'mah knock you out into East Jesus!" yelled Justin Mack, running across the yellow tiles, his henchmen on his heels.

"You said it!" laughed Katrina.

With a single stroke of the mop handle, I knocked the pipe from Justin's hand and sent him sprawling against the far wall.

Katrina swatted away the weapons of Derek and Dirk. It was clear to me that Katrina could have killed them both. In far less time than I've taken to tell it, the three punks were reduced to writhing blubber, moaning at our feet. We found ourselves masters of the downstairs bathroom.

III

The President's announcement ended.

Principal Brodsky had provided his summary to the full assembly. I knew Ms. Starblue and Mr. Triassic would be looking for us.

Katrina and I were coming up the stairs and there were the student teachers. We held our boom and mop sticks across forearms in the ancient Lizardanian style of cradling weapons. Upon seeing them, we went to opposite sides of the stairwell and assumed Lizardanian defensive stances. That made them even more agitated.

"Your weapons will be insufficient to defend you," said Mr. Triassic, big arms folded across his chest, stretching his sleeves ridiculously. "This reveals your primitive side. Many hours remain until tonight's Presentation. You've lost every singing session! Your voices are harsh with fatigue. You're exhausted. Admit it to yourselves. Soon you'll be under arrest. Give it up! Don't you see how futile it all is? You have *no chance to win*. Take us up on our generous offer, one that stands in spite of your foolishness. Come with us now and live or welcome death at the hands of your own kind! They may just have orders to kill you on the spot. Your world knows now that the Twins are coming and have accepted fate — it is nature's way. Put your little sticks down. Come with The Thirty that have been chosen — take your place — we will save your families! They don't have to die for nothing. You've done all that could be asked of humans to do. Now, let this go," Mr. Triassic sounded so human, like a real teacher giving some sound advice. It sure sounded true, every word — but it didn't sound good, not good enough.

So tired, we barely noticed Justin Mack. His beaten buddies sped up the stairs, past us, by the student teachers, and gone, obviously on their way to find Principal Brodsky.

"You're selling yourselves short," ventured Katrina in *Universalian*. "To get to know us will improve your own lives."

"Improvement's not necessary. You, my dear, have always been too presumptuous," said Ms. Starblue.

"You'll see, after the others have saved us," said I, supporting my friend. My voice was raspy but the words were clear.

Footfalls from the hall were heard.

"You'll defend us?" asked Katrina defiantly, clutching her stick.

"You've taken much from our people already I see," Ms. Starblue said. "I thought you couldn't be taught."

"Then you'll keep them from us and get us back to Hard'ack Hill?" I asked.

"Certainly...NOT!" Mr. Triassic laughed loudly. "Do you think I want our race influenced? Thirty is really *more* than enough," and he turned in the direction of the sound of hurrying feet. "Gentlemen! Dear ladies! Your quarry stands here, *black with crimes.* Come and arrest them both!" The sound of rushing people could be heard.

Back downstairs! I thought to Katrina and leapt with her into the basement. The corridors were dimly lit and rarely traveled. We ran as fast, headlong, full-out. Our pursuers were just around the last corner.

Window, Brian, we need a window!

A door with a wooden sign marked **PAINT ROOM** met us. It was guarded by a mammoth padlock.

"Allow me," said Katrina, out of breath, still with her wits. She swung her stick not downward but up from the left to the right, grazing the lock. It shattered and landed with a clank on the linoleum floor. One of the government agents came around the corner, gun at the ready. I whirled my stick, its yellow paint streaking like a comet. It hit the agent's pistol which fell from his stricken hand—and discharged. The ricochet hit glass within the paint room. Before it did, the bullet went through my open coat. The agent felt his feet fly from under him, swept out by Katrina's swift blow from her mop handle. I grabbed at Katrina, pulling her.

"Halt, federal officers, hands in the air!" bellowed one of the team, only an instant behind his fallen partner. Katrina slammed the door and pinned her mop stick into a crack on the floor and under the door knob. No sooner had the brace been applied than the door was professionally kicked three times. But for the moment, the way was barred, the stick holding fast.

Out of the way of the door, they might shoot through it.

I thought we were suppose to be taken in for questioning before being executed, Katrina thought back at me, catching her breath, her long fingers across her knees.

We looked around.

The glass breaking wasn't a window. Stricken were the collection of Mason jars.

Door to the right!

"Are you certain they went this way?"

We froze. It was Mr. Triassic.

"Oh, here they are. Hello! Perhaps we can help, you see, we're their teachers," Ms. Starblue was with him.

Conversation ensued outside as the officers urged the teachers to leave. But the two disguised Lizardanians were determined to be helpful.

"We want you to catch them too, very disruptive students, and...and *at a time like this!*" said Ms.

Starblue. "It's clear the kids brought the lizard things here. And that's probably got something to do with the Twins, er...ah, those asteroids barreling down. It's obviously their fault. We can help!" she said with wild enthusiasm.

"Yes, and I use to open doors like this in a previous job as a, uh...*bill collector!*" and before the astonished officers could say anything, Mr. Triassic was at the door.

Quick, into the next room!

Running, we glimpsed back. The door hinges were snapped like a twig, the heavy door slapped against the opposite wall, obliterating the poor collection of Mason jars. It was total wreckage.

"Oh, you're still rather good at that! If the world should survive, you could get an additional job," said Ms. Starblue with a girlish giggle.

Windows! Thought Katrina to me. We threw the bolt on the door to the room. We were in the boiler room. I grabbed a rotten chair and shoved it under the door knob. A window within the room was large enough to crawl through, but only one at a time. It was the only way out. The door was tried by the knob.

That's not going to hold a Lizardanian either, thought Katrina.

No kidding. I'm behind the boiler, they'll chase after you once you're through. Head to the woods, get to Har'dack Hill, I'll meet you there — no time to argue!

With that, I broke the window with a board and helped Katrina through. She emerged outside the school but got a couple of deep cuts on her bare arms. I thrust her coat up to her and then dove behind the boiler. I was not a full second later when the door was smashed in. I dimly wondered if Lizardanians could see through solid objects, too.

The host entered and went immediately to the open window, through which a harsh winter wind was blowing. Whiffs of snow came in.

"They're outside, sir!" said one officer, straining to crawl out the busted window.

"Get up there, Bill, do you see them, too?"

"No, must be out in the parking lot. There's some blood up here. Could we get those teachers out, please, for God's sake?"

The party left immediately, two agents through the window. But I could sense that not all had left. There was no sound. I still felt I wasn't alone. I waited utterly motionless, wanting so just to sleep — I never felt so tired.

"They're gone, Brian. And now you can go, too."

It was Principal Brodsky.

"Sorry Mr. Brodsky, I wish I had time to explain," said I, rising from behind the boiler.

"I know why you don't," said the principal. "It's you isn't it, you and that Russian girl, Katrina, right?"

"Yes...it's us."

"Is it...very awful?"

"It shouldn't be. I'm trying to convince them to help us, to destroy these asteroids or tell us how to do it ourselves. We disguised ourselves to protect our families."

"Well, I didn't recognize you on T.V., if that's helpful. It's not going very well?"

"No, not really. It's like American Idol or something; they're judging us. And not just on our singing, but on the message. We had a choice, so we chose music."

"Tough freshman year, huh, kid?"

"Pretty much."

"You know, even in crazy times like these, freshman all over the country, all over world, are having a tough time. Broken homes, jobs and studying, drugs, poverty, bullies, hormones, pimples — we don't give kids any right of passage. It's not just you…you're not alone."

"I feel alone."

"I see you've had it out again with Mr. Mack and his friends. You propped a motorcycle engine over one of the student teacher's closets? If you weren't busy trying to save the world, I'm afraid I'd have to give you a week's suspension."

"Justin and his crew put that there to get back at Ms. Starblue. And don't tell my Mom. Getting suspended wouldn't do her good."

"Well…" Mr. Brodsky looked both kind of pained. "Listen, I'm not going to suspend you — consider it a suspended suspension. I want to tell you something before you go. It might mean something to you later on. What I told you before, about letting nature take its course…I was wrong about that. Sometimes it's good to interfere to make things better. What are these aliens called, again?"

"Lizardanians. But there's almost no time left. We're not allowed to sleep or eat. It's just impossible, it's too hard and I can't do it anymore." I felt I'd fall over, now that I'd slowed down.

"They won't let you eat or sleep?"

"Some kind of ritual," I said.

"That's right…I saw you and Katrina in the library and not the lunch room."

"I have to go, Mr. Brodsky."

"How do they know if you sleep, maybe I can watch over you?"

111

"I don't know how they know. But I think they will."

"Brian, look. I saw Katrina running out across the lawn and I yelled to her to get in my car, you know, my old Ford. She's there now and I don't think they saw her get in. Those student teachers, Mr. Triassic and Ms. Starblue, they've led the FBI people to Har'dack Hill. They're with those Lizardanians that don't want to help us, right?" He sounded concerned.

"They're more than that, Mr. Brodsky. They *are* Lizardanian. And definitely down with the ones that don't want to help."

The principle looked shocked.

"She's waiting. She needs you," he said finally.

"How'd they fool you?"

"How should I have known? They had credentials. I admit I didn't call their references, but you don't expect aliens to come to your door everyday. This is Vermont, after all. There are still people who don't lock their doors. Sorry, kid..."

"It's okay, Mr. Brodsky—they're aliens and what they do seems like...just...magic."

"Magic consists of all the things we don't understand. It's like luck, which is just preparation colliding with opportunity," Mr. Brodsky put his hand on my shoulder and I winced, this being the one hit by Justin's engine trick. He took his hand back fast.

"Sorry. How'd that happen?"

"The engine hit me, I was trying to push Ms. Starblue out of its way."

"Would it have hurt her, I mean, if she's one of them?"

"I...didn't think it through."

"'Just saw someone in trouble, Mr. Miller? I don't

know if there's any hope for you, boy."

"I've sung to them. I've tried everything I can think of. This time, I'm beat."

"It's okay to get beat, kid. But you're only defeated when you give up. Don't give up."

"Maybe. I've learned a lot in the last few days — maybe lifetimes of knowing, I can't believe it. I feel like whole civilizations and peoples and planets are rising and falling in my mind, in my soul. It's kind of hard to explain, in our language," I concluded heavily.

"When you're a teenager, no one understands what you're going through, certainly not the older generation. Maybe that doesn't ever change," mused the principal.

A beam of light, like a blade, from the sun came through the shattered window that served as Katrina's escape hatch. It did so now, lighting up the dusty room.

"I can see why they picked teenagers," he said.

"Why's that?"

"Every teenager has to carry a world on their shoulders. You can take it."

"Yeah. But that was because I felt like the 'man of the house,' you know? Dad's moved out and Moms needs me — well, I guess everyone needs me now. It's really too much — but I have to finish it." I ran past the principal intent on finding Katrina.

"Wait, Brian," Mr. Brodsky said. He threw his keys on the basement floor.

"Take those, kid. Take my car, you and Katrina. Keep driving until your engagement tonight. If you have to wreck it...then do it. I know you're tired. It's time, I'm thinking, for you to take risks. Big risks," Mr. Brodsky said this, looking at the floor.

"Such as, Mr. Brodsky?" I really wanted to know.

"Promise anything. You can't let those comets hit this planet. It will kill everyone...and everything."

"They say it will be quick."

"I wonder if they know."

"You do?"

"It's death, for everything, just the same. I've got grand kids and I want to see them grow up. They're making you account for our misdeeds, that much I understand from listening to their music. It's not fair, but neither is life."

"I've already tried all I know."

"You have to get them to make a mistake. You have to *guilt them* into helping us, Brian Miller."

"The ones we're fighting with, Mr. Triassic and Ms. Starblue, they seem to have no weaknesses! They're not sentimental. I don't know if guilt will work on them. The Lizardanians want to take thirty kids off this planet before its over, before the Twins arrive. I think that's about the extent of their guilt feelings."

"The Twins?"

"These asteroids are known as the Twins of Triton, they came out of orbit from one of Neptune's moons—Triton. And they are called Eirosa and Chirminian. They're locked in a gravitational field, like magnets."

"Could these, uh, Lizardanians defeat them?"

"Yeah, but they'd have to get their friends to help. And they have no interest in asking."

"Why not?"

"This is nature's way."

Mr. Brodsky ran a hand under his chin in consideration, "Keep going, Brian."

I picked up the keys.

"Be careful, son — but take chances. Roll the bones. Now, get busy."

"Thanks, Mr. Brodsky."

"I wish I could advise you about just what to do, but I can't...you'll have to find the way."

"But what if I lose?"

"We'd be dead before long, anyway. How long do you think it would be before some crazy dictator or terrorist group gets hold of a nuke or chemical weapon or something we sell them and then throw us all right back into the Dark Ages, even if these asteroids weren't coming? We've run our course, kid, we've been pushed to the abyss because our technology has outpaced our wisdom. I can tell, it's coming with or without these Twins. You're fighting on the last battlefield, son. We need these people, we need them on this planet. We're killing our environment and we're only learning more thoroughly how to kill each other, everyday. I wish I were young enough to help you. But my time's over...I...I'm done."

"Some of what you say...sounds like them."

"We've got a lot of good, a lot of love left on our world. Carry that message 'hear? And I know, when it's over...you'll be the one standing."

A helicopter droned overhead. Brodsky walked to the broken window and looked up.

"Friends of yours?"

"Of Katrina's, too, maybe — there seems to be a lot of Russians around. I better go. Thanks for the car — uh, no promises as to its safe return."

"None needed, Brian. And forget about luck. It's not a game of chance, it's a contest of spirit. You don't have to be stronger or smarter than them — just be yourself."

"I'll try," I told him. And I meant it.

"Promise you'll give it all you've got and I'll be satisfied."

"Promise. But please just keep it all to yourself, Mr. Brodsky. We want our lives back after this."

"Us, too, kid. And another chance."

"I had another problem—drugs. I've quit, they helped me there, anyhow."

"I knew about the heroin, son. And I knew you'd beat it on your own. You can handle this too…so handle it."

That surprised me, big time. He didn't turn me in, and he could have all the time.

"Thanks for not busting me."

"Sure. And…*sing well.*"

I ran down the hall and back up the stairs, out to the parking lot, hoping to meet no one. My luck—or whatever—held. Seeing the principal's car, I leapt into the front seat, without looking in the back. I pushed the key home. The engine roared.

"Kat, are you back there? You okay?"

"Katrina's safe and you'll be too, Mr. Miller," said a voice that was not Katrina's.

"Damn it!"

I stomped on the gas pedal, sending himself—and my passenger, I hoped—pressed back into the seat. The wheels spun on the snow and ice and whammed the car around in a donut. I jerked the wheel hard to the right, aiming for another car, a white one, at the opposite end of the parking lot. I hit it at full speed. I leapt from the car. Wrecked the poor car, just like I was afraid I would, five minutes after the borrowing. I heard the sounds of pursuit, shouts and heavy footfalls in the snow.

I ran. A voice behind me yelled. They told me to

stop. I didn't look back. A series of shots range out, it sounded like an Uzi.

Geezum, they're shooting at me, I can't believe it!

"Brian, here!" it was Katrina.

"Kat!" at this over-loud response the shapes through the birch, thin oaks and poplars began to become more clear — many, many running people. For a moment it looked like half the town coming through the snowy trees and fading light.

I took the time to embrace her anyway, so great was my joy at seeing her. Then, like two gazelles side by side, we sprang through the snow and up the hill.

"Whereja go?" I asked as we ran breathlessly along. I didn't even think to think to her.

"'Had to leave the car, they were close, run now!'"

"Brodsky tried to help you, then?"

"Yeah, he tried. I told him about you still in the room — come on!" it was hard for her to talk and run her fastest.

We heard a larger group of people actually in front of us, cutting us off from our route up the hill. Our coats were still unbuttoned and flew out behind us, so fast was our pace.

Then we stopped abruptly. Only a few stands of trees separated us from those coming down. And those behind were closing fast, guided by our footprints in the fresh snow.

"Ideas?"

"They're all in YOUR head, now," I smiled at her through the ice that formed around my nose and mouth.

"No time for humor," responded the girl harshly. Her green eyes were flashing in the last rays of twilight. Her wild hair as messy as ever (which it was!), all tussled by the wind. Darkness was falling fast, but not fast enough to cover our footprints.

"They'll find us now," said Katrina in a tired voice.

Think everything — now at least they won't hear us.

Do they know where we're going?

Who knows — my guess is yes as tipped off by Danillia and Soreidian — in a previous job, they tracked down escaped prisoners!

Voices were now clear — military voices.

If we've made any friends among them, now'd be the time —

Katrina interrupted my thoughts, brows knitted in fierce concentration.

I don't plan to give up without a struggle, and I'm apt to fight anyone, human or alien, the way I feel now, since they all seem to be in league. It's like the only people in the galaxy who want to save Earth are you and me. But I feel like they've taught me enough to take on an army. Why does everyone hate us when we're the only chance?

Not true — a few people under orders from those who don't understand, that's all...

Katrina reached down and struggled up two long branches, brushing the snow off. I could almost feel her frozen hands just watching her. They must have felt like ice. We hadn't even reached the spot where our warm robes were hidden.

Let's see how many we can take. She handed one stick to me.

The shapes ahead quickly emerged. We prepared ourselves to fight.

The original eight Lizardanians appeared before us. Their stern faces were almost a relief.

"You appear to have failed to convince even your own people of the justice of your cause. You insist on continuing to try to convince *us* of what your own don't believe? And what's this? These sticks yet AGAIN?!" It was Danillia speaking, looking right at Katrina.

The exhausted Russian shot back, "We have you to thank for this, Danillia."

"You're here aren't you? We could have prevented it," Loridian spoke up.

It was apparent that only seconds separated us from those behind.

Torrillian now spoke. "You're tired, you need to sleep. You've fought well and yes, you've favorably impressed us. We know your music now — we'd actually heard some of it when we found your planet's *Voyager* spacecraft during our approach to Neptune when we first learned of the Twins. Is not the salvation of thirty of your race — and keeping Soreidian's promise — enough for you? Accept what has been offered. Danillia and Soreidian have accepted."

"We thank you for your words, but not for what you consider to be generosity..." I began.

"You wish another Presentation with us?" one of the most quiet of the Lizardanians asked, one Korillia.

From the sounds behind, it was clear that only a few trees separated us now from the authorities.

"We do. We put you on your honor to guide us there — any place you'd like," said Katrina. "This time you'll see why we should be saved."

At that instant, a dozen men and several women fully outfitted for military operations burst in. They were stopped short by the sight of the Lizardanians, but with weapons out and aimed.

Danillia said, "I'm afraid the youngsters are coming with us again tonight. We'll bring them back tomorrow, perhaps," she was addressing the first of the soldiers. The reptilians began to head through the snow toward the departure site, with us teens in tow, as if it were just that simple. She spoke in *Universalian*, so I was sure her meaning was clear, if her words weren't.

"Stop right there! These kids are coming with us!" yelled the leader the group, assault rifle raised. I knew that if someone shot at one of the Lizardanians anything might happen. The Lizardanians, though, did not appear concerned at all.

"Leave us alone!" added Katrina in Russian, directed toward the Russian agents. A Russian voice from the group implored her to come back with them.

"You fools! You'll wreck everything!"

"If you fire those weapons, you may as well be firing at yourselves. The Twins will kill this world unless we get Lizardania to stop them. This is beyond following orders; this is about the *extermination of life*. Please, put those guns down!" I was nearly begging, expending precious energy in diplomacy that should have been spent later on my music.

There was a brief silence during the stalemate. Then the leader of the pursuit yelled out.

"Check your fire! Check your weapons! Just...just let 'em go."

Instantly, most of the weapons were lowered, metallic safeties applied, clips removed, red laser finders turned off, pistols holstered.

The Lizardanian group turned to regard the human who had spoken. They looked surprised. There was another awkward silence of many seconds.

In *Universalian* Torrillian addressed them.

"They will be yours soon. They are exhausted. What they reserve in energy will be spent. After tonight, they won't have the strength to continue."

The group of humans, local police, and agents of the American, Canadian and Russian governments stood in the woods, with their lips parted, a soft but chill breeze rustling through the frozen trees.

"Don't give up!" urged a few from the group, toward Katrina and I.

"Keep fighting, Brian!" someone else yelled. Another person echoed the sentiment and then another and another.

"Defend the Motherland, Katrina Ivanovna!" it was a female voice in Russian.

The team leader slung his rifle, walked up and through himself in the snow before me. He put a hand on each of my arms, looking up.

"Listen to me, kid. I've got children. Some kids, do you hear? One about your age. I want you to get these people to help save us. If you think you shouldn't come back with us now, that's good enough for me. Do whatever it takes, no matter what you have to do. Now, you go and do that now."

The soldier rose.

Katrina and I watched the humans slowly depart, again becoming but gray shadows through the trees once more. Then they were gone.

Brian, we have to sing tonight as no humans have ever sung.

Yeah, I feel that way too. Tonight's about all I have left anyhow.

My heart aches more than my eyes, I feel as though my whole country were crammed into my body, demanding that we fight to the end.

"How about an early start, Torrillian," suggested Katrina boldly. "It's Soreidian and Danillia that look exhausted, we want them to be spared the further hardship of waiting up late." Lizardanians had a fascinating way of expressing themselves when they were perplexed or surprised. And the six of them made this expression now, nearly in unison. They shook their heads rapidly from side to side while simultaneously moving their necks and heads backward. It was almost 5:30 p.m.

"If Danillia and Soreidian are agreeable..." Torrillian answered, looking around at his fellows.

Danillia spoke right up after a quick mental consultation with her partner.

"We would be and immediately. It's an ending we can all look forward to," she seemed relieved.

How much time have we got? Katrina thought to me.

Enough. But we need to pour it on early.

They'll be summoning up all their strength. How can we win?

I didn't think it because I knew she'd say no way; no way in the doomed world!

Katrina, I know what to do. They breathe our air.

What are you up to? So what if they breathe air or water or anything else? What kind of clue is that? You can't make plans on something so unimportant? Has the lack sleep, food, or maybe those awful drugs pushed you to madness?

We're made an impression, now let's figure out where they're taking us next.

"Where to tonight?" Katrina asked.

"It's your planet, should it matter?" Loridian was speaking now.

"We rather like the ocean," Katrina said.

Danillia and Soreidian immediately keyed on the remark.

"I think if they like the ocean that we should provide them an ocean setting — oceans are much loved by all races — though your oceans are too polluted to be really enjoyable," Danillia added quickly.

"Your instruments await you at the new location. Hopefully this will be our last encounter and you'll see the wisdom of accompanying us and The Thirty. Your families have been promised survival — I know that will make some of the other Lizardanians unhappy, but you'll find that we stand by our pledges, whatever they are, no matter what happens," said Direidian.

IV

Katrina and I arrived on a beach, all right. We were along the Mediterranean Sea, in the embattled country of Israel. Villages and humanity were beyond the dunes. The sand was white, giving easily under our feet. Several Lizardanian ships floated like any large boats out in the water, undulating and rolling with the waves. A long, shimmering barrier, much like the one established during the other musical interludes, was present.

Where are your glasses?

Huh? I felt like I was in a dream, looking around at the dark blue water.

You don't have your glasses on — where are they?

Um, well…I guess they're on my night table…a million miles from here.

An interesting gift from people who want us to fail.

And for you?

Me?

Your vision was fine, so what have you been given?
I don't know, Brian. I don't feel any different — just
tired and really hungry. I wonder if you could hold me
back from a dead fish if I saw one on this beach...
You ready?
I get a choice?
Nope.

We threw ourselves into our music. I did most of
the singing, but Katrina backed me up and often we
sang together. We played the strange, multi-
functional guitar-like instruments. The same
Lizardanians who judged us before stood on the
beach now. Danillia and Soreidian prepared
themselves for the breaks between our musical scores
to pounce on us on all kinds of issues. I defended
humanity's history, Katrina explained the capacity of
the human mind to master the complexities of time,
space and the highest level mathematics. The
Lizardanians had always voted by turning their backs
in unison. Finally, the music faded away, echoing
over the waves after three hours of continuous play.
The music was still something akin to operatic rock or
pop music, but the tone was far slower, much slower
and more somber, the pace measured. We had
slowed it down a lot from our opening night because
we were too tired to do more. The message of one
song went beyond words, but among the many
impressions from the music, very roughly, was this
selection:

We don't have explanations, for the coming, lonely
night...
But you know we're on a mission,
A mission you secretly know is right,
Why can't you wear kid gloves right now?
We'd go with you, if we could

You've sacrificed your sense of right
Because you think all you do is good

You're so full of light and might
You've chosen a path for us lined with death
But you and I take from this air, this star, the
     same breath
And only through us can you see what is really
     right

We all know it's just a hopeless fight, (to save
     Earth!)
You've kept us awake every single long night
All of your friends know what the Twins mean
     for us
And you dare to call our fate something right?

Make helping us something easy to do
Help us to help you
We share the galaxy's dust and we feel like you
You're so full of yourselves, you don't even
     know what is true

We voice a quality of Justice
We stand for a quantity of Light
Our voices are raised into this sleepless night
These are the voices of what is right

We demand a modicum (just a crumb) of Mercy
And a Dipper's worth of brilliant insight
(We need you to need us)
Gravity, distance, these don't change our voices of
 heresy
We want you to change how you look at what is
 right

We have a battle before us
Let's fight it together
There's nothing more we need do
Let's see together what is good,
And what is...*true*

At the end of that set, one of almost two hours, it was only Danillia and Soreidian who stood with backs turned.

At that moment of wonder and loss on the part of the former student teachers, another ship approached from the setting sun. This one was much sleeker and less angular than the ships assembled, one with exceptionally long wings and a single large engine of sorts, offset from the center of the craft, with long fins which appeared to rotate clockwise, then counterclockwise, in an irregular rhythm. It was bizarre and utterly arresting to watch this craft glide up to the beach from the sea.

The moon's three-quarters added to the illumination put out by the Lizardanian ships. Nothing like the music played by Katrina and I on those Lizardanian instruments had even been played before. Nothing like the poetry, composed in the most desperate circumstances imaginable, the biggest stakes possible, had ever been delivered. Our message, to the complete surprise of the former student teachers, was winning hearts and minds among both the Lizardanians and their friends.

The strange craft with the offset engine now revealed its new listener. Littorian, Lord of the Lizardanians (only in special times!), descended down a short ramp and into the gentle waves along the beach, his long robes billowing in the light breeze, the waves surrounding them, but not getting them at all wet. Danillia and Soreidian tried to turn the moment back in their direction. The new arrival did not seem to please them.

CHAPTER NINE
Trapped by the Desperation

Littorian was, like all Lizardanians, almost eight feet tall and looked rather war-like. Like any lion in repose, or perhaps a wise, solitary dragon atop his mountain stronghold, or like that Sphinx in nearby Egypt, he radiated great, but controlled power towards Katrina and me.

His scales glittering in the light of the rising Moon, Littorian seemed both dangerous and disarming at once. To me, he seemed somewhat more youthful than the other Lizardanians. Though exceptionally muscular, as if built exclusively for battle, we got no feeling of hostility from him, unlike the ex-student teachers. Also different from those two and the Alligatorians, he did not wear a sword, or anything that looked like a weapon. Most of the other aliens were carrying weapons.

Littorian wore a series of robes that were open at the chest and like those worn by us, completely covered the body. His long, large tail, however, was always visible, and he had it wrapped about him as he watched us.

I rapidly approached a tight band of conferring aliens.

Addressing myself to the Alligatorians, I threw myself at the three representatives whose names I knew from my Lizardanian lessons as Nobilian, Beterian and Larascena, new to us.

"Though we'd sought to sing to Lizardania, we must now explain our vision to the Alligatorians, I see, who obviously have their minds made up in advance of our music!" I simply shouted in *Universalian* directly at Larascena. Everyone was taken by surprise. But I knew what I was doing, and I knew the price I'd pay for it.

Immediately a debate began between myself and Larascena, much to the bewilderment of the Lizardanians, Katrina and every other watcher in the galaxy.

As we stood there now yelling insults at each other, tables were produced from the Alligatorian's ship and literature spread upon them, apparently in response to some rite or tradition that I unknowingly invoked. Also upon these long tables were immediately spread many weapons, both traditional and modern, some like those the Alligatorians already wore. Most of these tools of war had obviously not been used in millennia. They were brought out for ceremonial adornment—and those rare instances when challenges were leveled. Some actually had dust on them, taken from decrepit boxes. Long scrolls of ancient learning were scattered and I noticed the Alligatorian glancing at them as she spoke, as though for reference. The tables were made of a rock-like substance resembling marble, but with a translucent quality. I accused the Alligatorians of permitting an inexcusable crime against the interstellar community

by helping to bring about the destruction of
humanity.

Danillia and Soreidian could scarcely believe their
good fortune, nor hide their satisfaction.

The ferocious debate was now entirely conducted
by music. Katrina and I were playing several
instruments at once, not in a wild cacophony of
sound, but in a disciplined, tight and hauntingly
beautiful rhythm that enthralled every listener. I
knew the music was good, if aggressive and
somewhat mean-spirited. We would only address the
Alligatorians, and the Alligatorians demanded that
the Lizardanians step aside and let them engage us
with their own powerful music.

It came now to Larascena and Beterian, the two
Alligatorians singing and playing against Katrina and
me, that we were more than we seemed. We had
been exposed to learning that they, the
Alligoratorians, had never been offered. It was a trust
that I convinced Katrina we must now, like money
saved for a really rainy day, spend recklessly. We
traded the Alligatorians song for song, argument for
argument, giving as good as we got — better. I did
more of the singing, Katrina more of the playing of
the instruments. My tenor quavered now and again,
but was still clear above the deep baritones of
Larascena and Beterian.

None could fail to understand our message of
hope, love and endurance, even as we accused the
Alligatorians of being murderers. This Katrina hated,
but she did it and well — because I asked her too. Our
loyalty to each other went beyond blood or promise —
it was rooted down to our souls, our spirits
themselves were completely intertwined. Not even

the Twins could pierce our bond of total, mutual faithfulness.

Our accusations offended, but the strength of the accusation seemed to send all counter-arguments and the music of Alligatoria into the dust and sand of that Israeli beach, into the night. We went on singing and playing our Lizardanian instruments without a break. The Alligatorians responded and we fought hour upon hour.

Katrina's fingers ran over the instruments with near-perfect control. One of these was like a synthesizer, one like an electric guitar but with over fifty strings, each making a unique and subtlety unique sound. My main instrument was simpler — a bass was as complex an instrument as I could handle, even with all Katrina's couching.

The Alligatorians raged that humanity was too evil, too divided, too bent on their own destruction, too selfish, to be allowed to join the galactic community. Our ideas, they said, were too small to be of any use, our world too polluted to have anything of value to trade with others, and so on and on. But we seemed not to hear — we had our case to make and we would see it done, at any cost.

Everything is justified, said Katrina.

Very brief pauses between musical sets were used to recalibrate the instruments on both sides. We and Alligatorians were profoundly tired after four hours of intense musical argument, us more than them. Twice, so.

We calibrated the instruments with a early knowledge now mastered, realizing that only enchanting our alien audience would save our world. The shores of Israel looked beautiful, but neither of us gave time to take in the scenery, brightly illuminated by the dozens of alien ships. Katrina looked around at the Muslims, Jews, Christians and others looking down from the dudes at their exhausted, last hopes.

I like that--'Anything is justified.' Look up!

She did. The stars burned above, unimaginably hot in icy space. But brighter than all, coming from the direction of Draco the Dragon, the Twins appeared twice planet size at their distance.

'Must, MUST stop those asteroids, Katrina. They are the end of second chances, Kat.

I know, Brian.

These Alligatorians are not as strong as Lizardanians. They don't know how to fight like a Lizardanian. But we know how...

Katrina put her instrument down that she was calibrating and looked soberly over her shoulder at me. My teeth were clenched, a little blood trickled from one corner of my mouth, so dry were my lips. The corners were cracked, my eyes only slits. Katrina then looked over at Larascena who still stared at me, her light orange pupils seemed a pale flame. She looked like a mountain of muscle and power, her dark scales revealed not a hint of weakness. The thought of attacking a brick wall with bare hands was infinitely more appealing to Katrina, and to me. To fight such a creature was certain death.

My gaze turned to the table with the scrolls — and the weapons. Upon the table were swords, long, oddly shaped knives and several items that closely resembled hatchets with triple- and quadruple-sided blades. The weapons were not what one would expect, shining silver and steel…instead, they were all completely black, to include their hilts — a kind of obsidian that sparkled and shone in the various artificial and natural lights of the wild night.

They're alive, you know. They call to us.

What are alive? Katrina asked — but then she suddenly she felt it too. She got to her feet, in unison with me, our instruments calibrated, pushing back-to-back until we rose.

Those weapons are alive. They grow on a planet of black, and they rise from the very soil and they live on sunlight like…like plants…or us. You know it?

I know it, I know it, now. But Brian you've never used a sword, let alone that other stuff. And neither have I. Don't you think they laid it out just for you to take this crazy step? Oh, Brian, you're too tired, you haven't thought this through.

'Can't give it up. No where to retreat. No beach, after this one, to walk on.

Larascena recognized my look of determination. She had seen that look before. It wasn't often that such a creature would have to fight. And I knew she had crushed everyone she had ever fought before. You could just tell.

I love who you are, Kat.

You're a good partner, Katrina thought to me with infinite kindness.

We clasped hands tightly.

Then I broke from her and made a sudden dash directly for the table with the scrolls and weapons. Knowledge and death lay side-by-side. Could use of the one stop use of the other? I would soon find out.

I knew my every move was being witnessed. But it didn't burden me. I had made my peace, and I thanked the galaxies for my life. I knew it was now at an end.

I thought about Principal Brodsky and the old man's wisdom. I wondered if he could see me now, from his living room — only Mr. Brodsky would understand my next move. And he would know himself to be the author.

Every alien eye was on me. Every human eye was on me. And there were other witnesses, too. My hand was on the table. In a few seconds, Larascena was next to me. I burst out to the assemblage,

"Larascena and her people advance their candidature for butchers of the human race! This does no honor to either the galactic community nor to Lizardanians, neither here nor on their home worlds!" I said it in Lizardanian.

"You accuse without evidence! You use the language of Lizardania to distort the truth, to the ruin of the memory of your doomed civilization. You've chosen to defend a world whose natural course has run itself out!" Larascena was not in a mood to be further lectured.

My gloved hand flashed toward the table. Larascena instinctively countermoved—just like I knew she would. Like I knew she must. I just tried to remember that everything counted…on my enduring this. Larascena grabbed one of the long knives and thrust it in my direction, all in one lightning quick motion. The blade buried itself to the hilt below my ribs on the right side, the knife was twisted expertly and withdrawn. It was so fast I could hardly recall it happening. But the pain…was blinding. The scroll fell from my hands. After, so did I.

I

"BRIAN!" I said, running to my friend.

I ran across the sand and caught him in my arms. I pushed my diving body under his, cushioning the fall, but sand would have done my dear friend no more hurt. How could it have? It looked like a bomb had hit Brian's lower body. I pushed hair from around his eyes and forehead. My tears and my anger fought to be first at the surface. There was a roaring my ears. My doomed world watched, its hopes, crumbled...

Larascena shrank back from the table. The understanding that she had probably killed one of the Presenters might have set her mind to the consequences. Maybe she only meant to defend herself from...*a scroll*? I knew these blades were always poisoned, from my studies, as if such a thing were necessary. And I knew there was no Lizardanian—or Alligatorian—cure, even if I could control the bleeding.

"Brian, oh God, NO! Don't leave me..." was all I could think to say. I ripping at my robes and stuffed a make-shift bandage into the gapping wound. No one moved to help my poor friend.

The aliens watching took in the meaning immediately. Brian was dying—as was our world—for neither was there an antidote. The Twins were only the worst part of it. Humanity watched as their best, and *last* hope, was leaving them for whatever fate await the foolish, innocent dead.

Some of the aliens were already moving toward their ships and departing. Clearly it was over.

On the dune knoll, Littorian watched the departures.

Larascena looked like she regretted her acts.

But it was not enough for me.

II

"'Sorry Kat, guess I've messed it up for everyone," Brian coughed.

Blood came up and ran lazily down the side of his mouth, rolling down his chin. I wiped it back angrily. My own blood was boiling.

A rage seized me and took possession of my body, mind and spirit.

I let Brian slip gently to the soaking sand. I rose, my long white robe hovering around me, splattered with my friend's blood. The great crimes of Lizardania and their friends could no longer go unanswered.

Larascena stepped away from her comrades. Beterian moved to the table and came back with several weapons, in their scabbards and sheaths. In silence, he outfitted Larascena, who made no move other than to stare hard at me. But I was well beyond fear. Another Alligatorian came from their ship at a trot with an exceptionally long sword, at least six feet in length, a huge blade, in a silver sheath. The weapon itself was black as pitch, but gleamed like a storm. This was slung across Larascena's back. She was donned for battle, now with a second long knife like the one she used on Brian, and another strange looking device from the table — a three-bladed hatchet.

"They can't get away with this...this, this *mass murder*. And I won't let them," I said, looking at Brian in the sand.

At the table, I let my Lizardanian teaching guide me. As I looked down, I heard *voices!* The swords and hatchets were actually calling to my mind.

Pick me, Katrina — I AM vengeance!
I, young human, pick me and I will slay your enemy!
Your cause is just, you will be invincible and know
victory, lift me!
Face them with me — do and let them die!
Save your people with me, not him, young Russian!
Choose wisely — not her — avenge your world with me!
I can take the Alligatorian's life, select me, child, me!

My hands moved as with ancient knowing and experience to outfit myself. In seconds, I placed a sword at my side, two of the hatchets in my belt, a long sword across the back like Larascena's. The sword across my back nearly touched the sand behind me. They all coached me, told me that my cause was just.

Everything is justified.

I also slipped two long knives into my belt on the right side. I am left-handed, but the positioning of the weapons was whispered into my consciousness. I had lost my love, and I had visions of holding his lifeless body, like a silhouette, as the Twins ripped the world to pieces around us.

Anything. Everything. Justified.

I yelled. I yelled like something primal, backed into my cave, the blades the only justice. I held a long knife in one hand, my willing sword in the other. I wished to God as I ran toward my enemy only for the strength and skill to deliver death.

Without backing up an inch, Larascena met all seven of my planned swings with quick and determined counterblows. I could scarcely believe the power of each move. Larascena then roared on her own, a deafening noise.

"This will hurt—but you won't live to feel the pain," she hissed in *Universalian.*

A lesson from Lizardania ripped into my mind. I deflected a heavy left and downward thrust from the Alligatorian. I felt myself pushed back hard into the sand which gave no stability. Neither did my heavier opponent get traction.

Larascena steadied herself quickly and sent another blow, this time with her knife at my unguarded side. My right shoulder ripped, down to my upper arm, through cape, flesh, down to the bone. The pain was a horror, and I leapt instinctively back. My ferocious attacker, a mouth full of huge, six-inch teeth snapped at me. Now Larascena whirled her sword around faster than I could move aside. The blow was not clumsily aimed and even though I was leaping back, it was clear that my fighting knowledge was a few seconds behind the applied experience of the Alligatorian.

With inhuman agility, the Alligatorian caught me through the left side of the midriff, slashing deeply. I fell to one knee and knew instantly that the wound was very deep. Larascena again took advantage, striking me in the skull with her own head. I fell to the ground, blood my mask. My hatchet flew to the sand. Adrenaline wasn't enough. Another blow from Larascena sent my sword flying from my hand. Mind on fire, like my shoulder and torso, I knew it was done with me. Like Brian. Like my world.

I've lost for you Russia! I'm so sorry...I must...fall...

I was awash in tears and blood, my face streaked in crimson. How could I think about fighting someone like this, someone without weakness, a perfect killing machine? She was too strong for me.

None of the aliens made the slightest move to help me. Many turned away.

The Alligatorian, without remorse, brought down her sword yet again, clearly intending to split me in halves. I raised my knife with a dexterity surprising to my opponent, shunting the other's blade into the sand. Life in me demanded I fight to my end. Larascena roared again the same, deafening war cry. She spun and hit my still raised knife with awesome force. The blade whipped away in a wide arc, close to the invisible barrier that marked the Presentation grounds. Neither of my hands now held a weapon.

Larascena gathered up my hair, jerking my neck down. She lifted me from the sand with ease, to better remove my head…and my suffering. She swung down upon me, and I saw a terrific light. But it was not the Light of Death.

Before Larascena could strike my neck, the Alligatorian was hit from her right by a human missile, my Brian on top of her. The brilliance from the crack of his sword on Larascena's descending blow lit up the night. Larascena screeched with surprise, but not from pain. Brian, bleeding steadily but with an obsidian sword in each hand, assumed the classic stance of a Lizardanian at combat. My pride swelled and I pushed my death away, in the sand on my knees, watching with wide eyes. He chose to spend himself at the end on me. Larascena got angrily up. She threw sand behind her in frustration.

The Lizardanians were shocked that my dying defender had become master of one technique. Brian was determined that his death should be costly to Larascena. He knew that aiming a blade up and along the scale line would count. I knew it, too. But the doing was something again. Head-on thrusts to the impenetrable scales where useless, but beneath them, flesh clung to muscle and bone like any other mortal creature.

Larascena came quickly with very heavy blows. Brian parried these, but he could not stop them. I watched; and rested. And I gathered myself. Each of the Alligatorian's thrusts pushed Brian back into the shifting sand. He fought hard; as hard as an American can fight.

Blows were exchanged with blinding rapidity. Brian's application of his newly mastered skills was proving something of a match to Larascena. But he was so badly wounded, Larascena unharmed and fresh. She did not understand the Lizardanian moves being applied against her. Larascena never came to blows with a Lizardanian. She did not know their art.

Brian's weapons helped him and gave him strength. But in a moment, his right hand sword was sent careening out of control toward a crowd of Parcharia. They moved, just in time, to avoid the weapon. Before Brian could even switch hands with his last sword, the hatchet of Larascena met the remaining blade with a deafening clang, like the ringing of a great bell. It knocked Brian over. Blade-first, it stuck out of the sand, the hilt waving back and forth like a sail in a storm.

Brian sank down. I knew he would not rise again.

Larascena saw this, too — but decided to finish him anyway. She raised her hatchet for the last time.

And that brought the fire out of me. The last of my dormant strength, a Russian's strength on the brink, I applied it all now.

I roared.

Larascena turned in shock, half-expecting a Lizardanian to attempt to hold her from her spent victim. Instead she saw me, only a wounded girl. But not just any girl, though. Not tonight. Such a yell could only mean I was now one with the Lizardanian art of war, as Brian had been—but certainly it was too late.

I leapt to my feet and flew over sand, armed with only a knife and a hatchet—I still had my long sword across my back.

You still can't accept nature's judgments, foolish one!

But I didn't answer. My weapons would speak for me now. Larascena took no alarm as I rushed toward her. She stared piteously.

Larascena threw her sword to the ground, shaking her great head. She was content with her knife and three-bladed hatchet.

Well, at least there will be some sport in this, armed with the same weapons, thought Larascena to me.

I watched her bloody knife, one oddly shaped at 90 degrees and hooked at the end, dripping with drops of my life.

I run over the sand in a fury. But it was not a flight of blind fury. I had learned the savage arts. I had become *savage*; blood-soaked, death-near, love-denied...a she-wolf. Running the black blades under the Alligatorian's scales were my one, primitive thought. The creature before me yet suffered nothing, possessed her full strength, was rested and alert. And overconfident.

As a world of humanity watched together with many billions of aliens through their representatives' transmissions across the cosmos, the Alligatorian swung her hatchet with unfathomable force and speed at me...

142

...and missed.

Larascena killed — the empty air. Where she struck, I was not.

Chest level to my opponent, I slid into the sand like a baseball player into home plate. My hatchet buried itself in the back of the Alligatorian, between the scales from the left hip to the right, unleashing a torrent of dark, bluish blood.

The Alligatorian attempted to hit me on both sides at once. Recalling my days in ballet, I blocked both blows, legs at 180 degrees, split to the sand, head arched back, the toes of my boots pointing upward to the stars. The move amazed all who beheld it.

I was slightly aware that two Alligatorians disappeared from their compatriots, dashing into their ship and reappeared moments later. They carried a huge device. It was like a long bow from the Dark Ages, but much larger, fully eight feet in length. The arrows accompanying it were only few feet shorter. Beterian made ready with this, but Nobilian stopped him with a glance. I could scarcely pay them attention.

Larascena's cries of pain and anguish from their fellow creature rent the air, positively shaking the entire Israeli beach.

On instinct, I turned the weapon to maximum advantage, slashing below the Alligatorian's scales. With my remaining strength, finding yet another vulnerable line of scales along the back, I dug the weapon in until the blade was completely buried. Then I leapt back, twisting and taking the weapon with me.

Not gods, nor giants...

—just flesh, blood, bone, mistakes and frailty hiding cowardly beneath dragon-hard scales. They weren't perfect killing machines intent on dining on human flesh. They were just people. But at that moment, I didn't care. Only vengeance and death could make it right. Whatever Brian was planning, it failed.

I glanced at Littorian. My position gave me a good view of him. His long, jagged claws were furrowed into the sand, the wispy seashore grass hiding his expression from me.

Larascena lashed out with her knife, again slicing through the empty air. She swore at me. I leapt further back, the loose sand alternating as ally and hindrance.

"You shouldn't swear—I don't abide it," said I to the creature in *Universalian*.

Larascena did so again anyway, shouting through her pain and surprise.

The creature's new defensive posture was instantly familiar to me. I remembered the countermoves. It was like recalling a dream.

I left my right side exposed and lashed with my long knife. I managed to lodge the weapon under the scales of the torso and I pulled hard and up, again twisting the blade while it was buried. The sand around us was very wet. Some blood was human, but most was not mine.

The creature lashed out with her tri-bladed hatchet and missed me again. I took advantage of her follow-through, hitting the creature in the neck with my own weapon, barely avoiding a tail swipe.

Unfair! I have no tail!

I barely avoided a handful of claws and another bite from Larascena's massive jaws. The crashing together of the teeth sounded like an explosion, inches from my right ear. The teeth would have

sheared through steel. I landed blow after blow
beneath the scales, blood spattering everywhere. My
own wounds were bound with pieces of my robes, an
act completed when Brian fought for me.

Larascena finally fell hard on her knees. She had
never known such pain. Watching her precious fluids
flow from a dozen scores and rips, I could see she was
summoning her vastly superior strength, resolved to
kill me once and for all. At first, she toyed with me.
But now the toy had turned the tables. As our blood
flowed together into the Israeli sand, more than one
alien witness looked shocked and ashamed. And I
didn't care.

Larascena gasped for breath. She swore once
again, this time at herself for underestimating me.
She was ready and pulled the long sword from the
sheath across her scaled back. Larascena forced
herself to her feet, towering above me. With her full
strength, which I knew could never be resisted,
Larascena swept the blade before her. Anything in its
path would be cut down. The battle would be over.
Nothing could stop her stroke.

Larascena swung the broad sword at hip level,
intent on slicing me in two. But I saw it coming.

I pulled my own long sword from my back and
placed it flat against my bloodied right side in a
single, smooth motion, snug to the hip bone.
Larascena's sword hit mine and sent me head-over-
heels. Pressed up against my own blade, I landed
directly back on my feet before the startled Larascena.
Years of state schools and the cruelties of gymnastics
taught under hard hands prepared me to land firm on
my feet. To rise up—and rose I did. I shut the pain
from my mind. The Alligatorian still followed her
sword blow around in a wide arc.

I then hit the creature in the neck again with my hatchet. Larascena fell to the ground, finally helpless before me, grasping her twice-wounded throat. There was so much blood, hers and mine, that the ground was squishing with it. My wounds were fatal. But she would go first...

I angled my sword into one of the dozen wounds on my opponent's broad chest. All there was left to do was shove. I leaned against the hilt to press down.

Littorian must have felt an all but irresistible calling to interfere, for he was now on his feet. There was an uproar among the Alligatorians who seemed about to come to the aid of their fallen comrade. So I knew only a moment or two remained to me to finish the creature before they were on me. I channeled my last strength to this well-deserved push. I wanted her to know why I going to ruin her.

And now you die, you damn ALLIGORATOR — because you killed...my...my love!

"NO, Katrina!"

It was Brian propping himself up with one hand.

"That's not what you're about! That's not why we're here!" he yelled it in Russian. But I wanted so to finish my butcher's work.

"Don't kill, Kat! Show...them what...mercy looks like...since they've forgotten." Brian's breath ran out. But I heard him. And I knew that he was right. This was not what I was about. Mercy. Mercy had to be shown by someone first. I bowed my tired head, realizing it must be me. My hair, wet with sweat and tangled by blood and severed skin--I knew I looked like a nightmare. And I didn't care.

One spark of decency, against this hopeless night, set against the certainty of a destroyed world.

Reluctantly, I pulled back on the sword, dislodging it from a wound beneath Larascena's chest scales. I looked over to my fallen friend, blood caked on the ground.

I turned to the tight knot of Alligatorians, huddling in silence. Behind them another alien ship was breaking from deep space travel, shimmering as it materialized, slowing, hovering above the waves, closing on the scene of the carnage. The barrier established to keep back the humans back, parted for the new ship. It was a long craft with a large offset engine, like several others in the area. Brian saw it too, but he was too tired and close to death to appreciate its beauty. The ship was white, like the snow back in far away Vermont or Russia — places we'd failed to save. And that was worse than the physical pain from the weapons and their poison that ran in our blood. Every new born bird, crying baby, every whale, and eagle in her lonely nest…would pay too.

I dragged my sword behind me, staggering over to my friend. I paused long enough in front to the Alligatorians to throw it at them. Their astonishment was apparent — and shame complete. Yeah, better be. I cared not about the shocked gazes following me.

I sunk down beside my friend. Then I looked up at the approaching Twins, glowing brighter and larger than ever. The contrails winded out behind them, like a nightmare. Those beacons of destruction were set on crushing a shiny jewel that was my world. And my swords, laying in the sand, could do nothing to prevent it. I propped Brian up once again, running a hand through his black, wet hair.

"Brian…can you hear me?"

He had blood on both sides of his mouth. His

147

eyes were closed, his once full lips, bloodless.

"I'm with you Kat," whispered he in Russian.

"We've made a mess of this," I answered.

He did not reply.

"Why, *why*! Why did you do it, Brian, bring us all to death like this?"

"I thought," he said weakly, "that if they jumped us for no reason we…we could *guilt them into helping us.*"

"Well that was pretty crazy," I said, wiping blood and perspiration from his forehead with my long sleeves.

"'Didn't think it'd turn out like this. Exchange forgivenesses with me, Katrina, here at the end."

"You hid your plan from me," I scolded, unforgiving.

"I thought you'd try to stop me if I told you."

"Don't ever hide anything from me again, okay?" I wanted a promise, as my long hair brushed close to Brian's cheek.

"Never again…I liked being with you Kat, and kissing you in the snow in that ditch back in town, a million years ago…"

"A trillion years ago."

"I have failed you…for—forgive me." And laying there, these were the last words Brian spoke on the crimson beach.

"I…I…forgive…."

Four aliens approached. I assumed as much of a defensive posture as I could muster, still on the ground with Brian's slumped head in my lap. I prepared for the end. I decided the final blows would be aimed at the Alligatorian coming since it was that race that had caused me the most suffering. The Seree were an incredibly strange looking group of

aliens, even for aliens. It was hard to even look at
their faces which were misty and as light as snow.
They were tall and wore robes like those given to us.
The hue of the skin, the perfect whiteness of snow,
almost seemed transparent.

"That's far enough," I told the group, brandishing
the knife.

"No harm is meant to you," said the Seree in a
voice that sounded like *Universalian* but more
musical.

"That's obvious," I said with sarcasm, in
Lizardanian.

"Death need not be your fate." It was Littorian.
"We will help you and your world. We have no
interest in your future sacrifice. Your music has
reached us. Your courage has moved us. Your spirits
are strong. We have been wrong, wrong to force you
to this. The Seree will help you step from the Dark
Edge and keep you in this life, with us, if you but
permit it. Leave not, with your work undone. Please
lower your weapon and let the Seree help you, as
only they can."

The words sounded too good to be true.

I dropped the obsidian blade, but only because I
could hold it no longer. I sunk to the sand, and the
stars above were all I could see.

I was lifted up and placed bodily on something
hard but incredibly smooth and comforting, and I felt
Brian's hand slip from my fingers…and then I ceased
to feel anything.

CHAPTER TEN
A World's Last Dream

I opened my eyes. They seemed glued shut. I expected to see Katrina. A white ceiling came into focus. It was not a Lizardanian or alien spaceship's ceiling...it just an acoustic, tile ceiling. I was propped up in a bed—a hospital bed in a semi-private room. I was not aboard some starship headed for a beautiful planet of an advanced civilization. I sat up. The room was warm, and a Vermont winter reigned outside a large window a few feet from my bed. At the moment, the sky was clear, but much snow, I could see, was down. I felt at my chest. No upside down sailboat hung on a chain about my neck. Neither was there a scare on my ribs where an Alligatorian blade might have left some huge marks. And my shoulder, in various levels of pain since the engine fell on it back in Ms. Starblue's class, no longer troubled me. If there at been an engine at all!

I hit my head...and it was...just a dream? It seemed...as real as...real feels...

Then I noticed a pile of newspapers on a table beneath the window opposite my bed. As I rose quietly, the room remained silent. I slowly drew the curtain to the bed next to mine, half expecting, half fearing to see a Russian girl laying there.

The bed was made—empty. Beyond it another curtain was drawn and maybe another bed was situated close to the door—but the newspapers!

My feet were bare, but the floor was not cold. It occurred to me that every newspaper in the world, every magazine covered the story of the century, the story of all time, for that matter—the story of Katrina and Brian!

If it happened, it'll be in the papers — the whole world was watching...

I went quickly to the pile of Vermont newspapers and national media magazines. I scanned the headlines quickly. Wars in the Middle East, tax problems, destroying the welfare state, global warming and climate change, failed crops, local politics, national politics, globalization commanded by multinationals, celebrity politics—and more celebrities! No word about asteroids on a collision course with Earth. No mention of two teens fighting to get aliens to save it. No mention of a Russian girl named Katrina, a lovely girl, a noble girl...a girl now a prisoner of my dreams alone. Snippets of song came to me then, but again, song only sung while asleep. At this my heart fell. Such a dream to make one feel so strongly about another human was...just like a crime.

I dropped the papers heavily, just threw them all down, my anguish complete. I was alone again, with my work after school, with my mom, with myself. With...my drugs? I recalled the urge, but it seemed distant. Outside, there was new snow, but I turned away without looking at it, letting the last of the magazines slip through my fingers. I looked at them laying there on the hospital's white-and-black checkered floor, wishing they said something different. Not a single caption bore the name Brian Miller…nor Katrina Ivanovna Chakiya.

"I wanted it so much…for her to be real…" I murmured, now possessed only of the thought of getting back into my bed. At least the world was safe.

"Those're old. You should have checked the dates."

I continued to stare at the papers on the floor.

It was a girl's voice, a Russian's voice, from around that last curtain.

My head jerked back with a snap. Flying across the room to the veil, I wrenched it back violently.

There was Katrina, propped up with several pillows, a book in her hands, and several others piled up next to her.

"I always wanted to read these in Russia, these *Harry Potter* books, but never had the time. Waiting for you was just the thing. This kid seems slightly less crazy than you — I can identify with the girl — why is it that she's the only one who has to read the magic books? How do the boys learn their spells, all stupid like they are? Why is everything hard to pronounce, like the girl's name? Why aren't you answering any of my questions? I wonder what she needs these guys for at all!" And she winked at me.

"Katrina!"

"No need to yell, I'm sitting right here, silly. Down, boy."

"It happened!" My heart leapt at the hard reality…and the possibilities.

"Well of course, what did you think, that you could have dreamed it? Please. Well, I forgive you, at first I thought the same thing. I looked at those old newspapers laying there, they fooled me too when I woke up. At least I didn't throw everything everywhere. Then I saw you. And them. There've been doctors and aliens in and out of here since we got here—but they wouldn't let our doctors treat us, 'said they knew better. They said it was best to wake on our own and not be too shocked by seeing them right away. So here we are!"

The girl had to endure me catching her in an embrace, falling against the bed, kissing her warm cheeks and hugging her closely. And I admit, as I remembered the hours on the Israeli beach, I wept into her shoulder for a time. She returned the pressure, stroking my hair.

"Hey, hey, settle down, I'm all right. Oh, now don't cry!" she whispered, caressing my neck— "people'll be in any second, 'wouldn't want them to get any ideas," and then she laughed carelessly. But she did not let go her firm grip on the back of my neck, just the same. "My Dad's around, and he'd better meet you first before he sees us like this."

"The comets are real?"

"All too. Look out that window." Her voice was more somber now and I went to the window. I looked up at the patch of blue sky, between some large gray clouds heavy what would soon be snow. A star defied the extinguishing light of day. It hung in the air, burning bigger than Jupiter on a clear night. A thin, white streak spread out behind it.

I moved back to the bedside of my friend.

"They'll help us?"

"Lizardania and their friends are going to meet soon with the heads of the world's governments and especially with the militaries. But they want us by them, as the languages they've learned from us are still a little challenging for them. All the countries with nuclear weapons will be turning them over to

Lizardania. The rockets will be fired into space at the Twins. Guess we finally stumbled on a way to be rid of the damn things and for a good cause, too."

"You swore," I smiled.

"Ha, so I did...Papa hates that...again, it's your fault. Say, I have something that belongs to you," and Katrina held our a silver chain, with a medallion hanging from it.

"Well, we have a chance!" My enthusiasm was rising as I put the chain around my neck.

"Thanks to you and your crazy plan. You *guilted them* into this, alright. We didn't win fair and square. I *might* forgive you, since that was the only way."

"Yeah, thanks. I'm sorry I didn't tell you. Really."

Katrina took my hand. "Forget it, 'more important stuff going on. Our robes are in this closet — we have new ones, these ones from the Alligatorians, not the Lizardanians or Seree. They've even more beautiful than the last. I guess the Alligatorians feel more *guilted* than anyone. And they should! I was waiting for you before trying them...bathroom's just there, ahem, you'll want to freshen up. Hurry up now...the world's waiting for Brian Miller," she smiled at me, looking just a little sad. "Lizardania insisted on our being left alone until we were both on our feet. Now we can see our families — ours have met, I hear."

I did what I had to in the well-stocked bathroom, loving the warm water.

Leaping into my new robes, they were more complete, more comfortable than any clothes I'd ever known. They had blue sleeves, a dark brown interior and a green and yellow-gold outer material.

"Careful now, we're on public display again once we walk through that door," said Katrina, adjusting my garments and eyeing me critically. Katrina wore the same striking colors. They weren't "loud" colors—but they whispered insistently.

Can you still hear me?

Da.

Don't leave me.

Nevermore.

Katrina opened the door. A crowded hallway greeted us with thunderous applause and cheering. I prepared myself to be embarrassed, but not well enough. Lizardanians and several Alligatorians, Seree, Parcharia and Orcharia came over to meet us, as did our family members, all tears and cries of joy and hope. Various human officials and the media were also awaiting us. As they gathered around, I looked over the crowd to a far window. A light shown in the sky—but it was not the sun. It was a death light.

CHAPTER ELEVEN
The Twins of Triton

All the aliens communicated only with
Universalian or their own languages and only through
Katrina and me. The Twins picked up speed due to
gravitational forces that I could only understand after
Katrina's repeated mental tutoring.

Katrina and I stood in Taylor Park, a few blocks
from the hospital. We spoke to Littorian, out in the
snow. A respectful distance away, humans and aliens
awaited direction from the Lord of Lizardania — and
us teenagers. Closer, officials from many countries
stood anxiously, wishing that strategy discussions
could be held indoors rather than in Vermont's
inhospitable winter. The three of us liked the
outdoors best, whatever the weather.

"We require you to turn over control of all your
planet's weapons — everything and immediately. Do
you accept?" Littorian's question was directed at the
two of us.

"The militaries of your world must cooperate
with our people and those of our friends. The
Parcharia have not agreed to help and have left. Their
delegation could not make a decision about

intervention. But we need them to ensure that the Twins can be destroyed. Even your planet's weapons, enhanced by us, may be insufficient, I fear."

To gain time while mentally discussing things with Katrina, I pointed out to the Lizardanians that across the street from the park was the site of the northernmost Civil War battle. The "St. Albans Raid" had been carried out by Southern sympathizers. We walked through the snow, and thank goodness the sun was out and bright, giving just a little warmth to the masses of people a respectful distance away. The Lizardanian looked up at the plaque marking the spot.

"What does this mean, this 'Civil War'?" asked Littorian.

Katrina answered, which relieved me greatly.

"This country had a great crisis, once. It's was divided by regions over some important social and economic questions," she said guardedly. I was thinking to her that the "peculiar institution" of slavery might be too heavy a concept for this particular moment. Katrina looked into the heavens at the star that shone even in the full daylight.

"If we get the chance, we'll tell you about it," said she, trying to stay focused.

"There is much uncertainty in this, if you make this world your final stand," said Littorian looking down apologetically.

"We already made that choice, if you please, my lord. You mean we may not be able to destroy the Twins?" Katrina asked.

"All your nuclear missiles will have to be improved to support our efforts. From our observations, your people have destroyed many of these weapons, many others are not usable. The

Twins are not rock—they are composite metals and mineral fragments that will challenge your atmosphere to burn them and all our combined weapons to destroy them."

"What can we do to help?" Katrina was renewed, rested and ready for action.

"The Parcharia were impressed with you—they told us so before they left. They have weapons that Lizardanian starships lack. But neither of the Starfinders live for massive destruction—they live to travel. We have rarely needed powerful weapons possessed by others, like the Parcharia. They are more adventurous than are we—some sections of our galaxy are a little...more primitive than others."

I'm not following everything he's saying, Katrina thought to me.

Neither am I. We'll have to figure it out later. What's a Starfinder?

"You," Littorian went on, turning to Katrina, "touched the heart of the Seree, so they saved you. Larascena is fortunate in this way too, for she too would have died without their aid! All respect you, Katrina, as a great warrior. Brian, I'm afraid, has earned a somewhat different reputation and he should not go to the Parcharia, if you would take my counsel. Your act...was not rational," concluded the Lizardanian looking at me in a rather disapproving way.

"Well...that's what I thought I needed to do. Our world would have been destroyed anyway, so I had to do something. So I just did it," it seemed pretty simple to me.

"Maybe. And maybe again you didn't have anything figured out at all, and simply got lucky," said Littorian, narrowing his eyes. Katrina couldn't help smirking. I felt my mouth drop open—but only for a moment.

The Lizardanian idea of luck sounds like ours, Katrina thought to me.

Luck, my Dad use to say, is the 'inexplicable favor of God,' I thought back.

Inexplicable is…unexplainable, yes?

Yup.

Ah-ha. I think they do have your number, Brian Miller.

I hope you learned that expression from me.

Yup.

"The Parcharia know the art of war the way the Seree know the art of healing. Torrillian will go with you and appeal to their people in their Great Hall—a hall from which you can address their entire world, over 100 billion spirits—ten times your population here. Without them, we may well fail to stop the Twins from reaping unspeakable damage to your planet, a world whose resources are already strained due to your people's poor management," he added the last with some indifference, stinging the two of us. But we knew it was true.

"You're right about us there," was my response. "But you'll see a big change now that we know how fragile our world is. And we want to learn how to preserve life here."

"It may be a lesson learned too late. We'll soon see," said Ettoros in a dismissive voice, standing near.

"They must send their best starships and war platforms. And they might need to bring the nets, so remind them, Katrina," said Littorian, taking no notice of Erroros' remark. Littorian looked up at the bright star that wasn't a star, glowing in the sky. It was midday yet the Twins burned and seem to grow in size by the moment.

Nets? What's he talking about? And Platforms?

I think you better just bring them.

Nets, seriously?

That's what he said!

"Katrina has a mission," I said to the group. "What is there for me?"

"You," Littorian turned and put a huge clawed hand on my shoulder. The gesture was both comforting and enormously intimidating. "You must help me to keep Ettoros, Direidian, Loridian, Danillia, Soreidian and the others focused. Each of the remaining pieces would destroy much. They must be diminished before they hit your world, particularly the largest. Some will be as wide as a mile across even after the battle. Lizardania is with you. You must put yourself wholly into the task," Littorian told me.

I know about your recent experiences with these substances — and I think I know who helped lead you to them. Of that, another time.

I was shocked, but let Littorian's thought go for the moment...the world's challenge, not my problems, mattered.

"The cost of this defense may be higher than any of us can guess, but you have been pledged the support of Lizardania, Alligatoria, the Orcharia and the Seree — if Katrina comes back with the Parcharia, I know your people will survive. Hold to that. Such pledges are not given lightly. You asked for a chance. You have that chance. It is almost time to say your good-byes. Time is indeed short!"

Katrina squeezed me so tightly as we embraced.

"Ouch—hey I'm on your side, remember?" I smiled as Katrina decreased pressure.

How are you feeling?

Hey, I'm outrageous. I've got this worked out now…it's this mission, that's my drug, I swear. I'll never despair like that again.

I'll be there for you Brian.

All the alien delegations had strode from the hospital in the snow before the bewildered human onlookers. Taylor Park had never seen a more unusual gathering. Nervous police and Vermont National Guard troops circled the officials and the aliens, ready to keep the curious crowds back. But people were not boisterous, nor pushing forward. They just wanted to see.

"It is time for Katrina to go to Parcharia."

"We must leave," said Torrillian, looking over to Katrina with a nod.

"We'll see you soon. Depend on me."

I kissed her gently on the cheek, a snowflake landing just on the spot as I withdrew from her gentle warmth.

Slashing away tears, she whirled away, her long cape billowing out behind her.

Torrillian and Katrina headed for the town baseball diamond near the railway. It hosted the Lizardanian ship *Echo,* a small craft, but impressive in both beauty and speed. A crowd of people were tolerated to caress the ship, admiring its smooth surface, quite pleasantly cool, not cold, to the touch.

I watched them go and then turned to Littorian.

"How much time?"

"If you mean you and I, I was hoping you might know."

"No, I mean how much time does my world have?"

"Ten rotations — I mean days. About." The Lord of the Lizardanians, looked up at the Twins in the cloudless, cold sky. He sighed, folded his arms and then looked around the winter landscape in the small northwestern Vermont railroad town, and toward the human military and civilian officials. He appeared to assess his defenses.

"Much to do," said he quietly. "The Twins will pass Jupiter's outer moons in hours." Above, a streak of light and a thin vapor trail slashed the blue, and then were gone. My thoughts followed Katrina.

"How long will it take to prepare?" I asked, forcing back the lump in my throat. What would a commanding general say? I searched my mind for everything in Lizardanian history that I could recall about their military commanders. They didn't have many.

"I have a plan, but your world — all your people must cooperate. Do you think they can forget their differences long enough to save themselves?"

"I think they will."

"Many of my people doubt it. All your resources, your weapons, your scientists and engineers, your young and old and all between — everyone must contribute to this effort, they must obey Lizardania over this very small time. They must move, they must think, as one — one struggling for life. Will they?"

I knew there was but one answer to give. And I hoped I wasn't lying.

"Yes, they sure will," was what I said. I hid my doubts.

I detected more than a little doubt in the low,

throaty rumble.

I thought fast. "I need four hours."

All nodded assent. I found it interesting that the aliens seemed to process *Universalian* in roughly the same way, though the Seree appeared to nod sideways.

"May Soreidian go with me?"

"It would be an honor. You have my protection and approval. I wonder, though, if it would be easier for your people to see Mr. Triassic than me."

I collected myself and looked around. A respectful distance away, beyond the police and National Guard troops, I could make out some family members, friends from high school…and some old enemies, too. But for now, I would have to think only of the Twins.

The other aliens, including Littorian, then abruptly left to wait aboard their command ships.

I walked straight away to the police line and to those officials who, though wide-eyed, appeared to be in charge. I saw a man in uniform and recognized him from the headlines as the Adjutant General of Vermont. General Dubie watched me closely. Not tall, but very dignified, I decided to talk to him before anyone else.

"We need to meet at the United Nations building in New York City," I told him, with as much ceremony and authority as I could muster. "Please meet us there with, well, all of Earth's leaders," Before he could answer, I turned quickly to Soreidian.

"We need to go there…" and when Soreidian only stared at me, I said, "Can we go there?"

In minutes we were walking from Soreidian's small personal spacecraft—a beautiful, silver ride, roughly the size of a few cars end-to-end—and up the stairs in the front of the United Nations Building. A crowd of police gathered and escorted us (from a respectable distance).

"Excuse me...which way to the General Assembly?" I recalled my civics class, and the guard I spoke to led the way. Officials split the sea of people before us like icebreakers, waving those away who would impede our progress. Badges were flashed, credentials exchanged, television cameramen frantically jockeyed for position, and I was ushered to the required podium. The hastily assembled delegates, representing the world's nations, faced the rostrum, taking their seats in a rush.

With Soreidian at my side, I knew there was no time for fear. I began to speak into several hastily arranged microphones. Intimately singing in front of aliens seemed far easier, particularly when I knew that I couldn't be recognized. I talked for an hour, without notes, and I wasn't going to take any questions. I told all humanity to defend the planet by listening to *and obeying* the Lizardanians and the aliens now obliged to assist us. I told them it was the only way we would survive as a race.

I

Narrative Taken Over By Katrina's Father

General Petrovich sat shocked as any of us in his crowded Kremlin office, staring at the television, listening to an American teenager asking Russia — and every country — to immediately surrender all nuclear weapons to the aliens. I hoped I wouldn't have to fight him to convince him that if Brian Miller asked it, life depended on a quick, affirmative answer. The general grimaced when he heard that a strategy would be dictated by the reptilian creatures. And their instructions must be followed to the letter, without question. It seemed like a chapter from a science fiction book had been borrowed in reverse.

But with Russia's new pride and joy suddenly off to another planet to get more help, my general's suspicions were kindled.

"ALL weapons? Didn't they try to kill Katrina?" General Petrovich and General Krohotkin stood immediately.

Our President sighed at them. She stood, and looked out her window at the burning dot in the sky. The sun was unobstructed by clouds, the Twins were horrifying and insistent.

"The alternative, the end of all life, is somewhat… um, *unpleasant*," said President Kollanti to her generals.

"Can we believe this Miller? He says that Katrina has gone to get more help?" General Yahzov asked.

"Can we afford to spend even one more minute in doubt, Yegor Illyitch?" I asked. I had been brought in the evening before for consultations. We had been up all night talking it over. I feared no general's wrath for my candid tone. With the President there, I knew I had to be frank and insistent.

"My daughter knows what she's doing. She showed that to the world. And I think this Brian Miller knows, too. Madam President, I say we should submit to the Lizardanians. It is the only road to survival!"

There was a pause before the president replied.

"The ambassador is quite correct. We have an obligation to the unborn of Russia and all nations. Let's have a teleconference before the Americans and get out in front of us again. Submit to everything, my dear generals. Everything. I announce the same and your complete cooperation in ten minutes!" President Kollanti never sounded so sure. Eight minutes later, she was addressing Russia and the world on television.

II

At the White House, I watch Littorian handling a shadow box containing an antique Civil War revolver. He took the weapon out of the box and examined it, rather awkwardly.

"This Civil War of yours, Brian...I find myself very curious about it. Far away and long ago in our history, Lizardanians had a similar conflict, with one of our cousin-races. For us, though, the conflict has never ended! We are far fewer in number than our enemy. When this is finished, I should like to start my detailed education of your world on this matter. Perhaps we can learn how to end our own war, which has gone on for eons of time." He set the weapon back in its case. The motion brought some relief to several officials in the room, I could see. I figured the gun was empty, and shrugged off the sighs I heard around me.

The President, with a large following of assistants, generals and international officials, came into the crowded Lincoln Sitting Room. My requested four hours were now history.

"America and, I'm sure, the whole world pledges 110% support," said the President, and he held out his hand. I quickly thought the appropriate response to Littorian, among the first of our mental communications. The creature shook the President's hand, being exceptionally careful, fortunately for the President.

CHAPTER TWELVE
Reigning in the Storm

I

"Our defense against Eirosa and Chirminian will take all the effort of Lizardania, the great Orcharian metacruisers, the gifts from the Alligatorians, the Seree's battle platforms and the Parcharia, too. Without the Parcharia, victory is doubtful — your planet may still be ruined," Littorian looked around the Pentagon's large basement conference room also knows as the "Tank". The "platforms," as it turned out, were pretty much space aircraft carriers, very flat, and multi-decked to carry many fighter craft.

The Tank was filled to capacity. The final plans would be made here at the Pentagon, the Saint Albans City Hall war room now moved to a more appropriate setting. Three days of feverish work were gone. People were tired, but alert. For three days, I had not slept either.

"You humans will see yourselves rid of the nuclear weapons you have so long feared — and coveted. Perhaps you have mixed feelings about this.

I've seen in Brian's mind that it is these weapons that have kept you from the kinds of wars you once waged. That may be true, but there's no time now for me to investigate it. Katrina and Brian have shown us your worth through their willingness to sacrifice themselves for you. They could have left with us," Littorian looked toward me with unabashed admiration. It was terribly embarrassing, but hard as it was, I didn't look down, because there was nothing to be ashamed of. I did what had to be done, from the quitting drugs to a sword fight I knew I couldn't win.

"Please direct your attention to this screen. We will soon see the results of your work, and ours together," Littorian told his audience. Ettoros stood by, holding a small device, affixed to what seemed like a little dish antenna, and spread some stabilizing legs of the device out on the conference table. So large and powerfully built a creature handling what appeared by his movements to be an incredibly sensitive device, fascinated all of us.

Even without the lights dimmed, a screen suddenly came alive in three-dimensional images of perfect clarity. The Twins, Eirosa and Chirminian, confronted the group. They were dark, with white ice on their edges. Eirosa was slightly ahead of its mate, crushing through space debris and pulverizing all in its path. Eirosa was an incredible 83 miles long and as wide, Chirminian just under 50. They seemed bigger.

"They will obliterate all life on this planet within a day of impact. Some of our more scientific minds believe your world will be severed by them because of their speed and composition. Think of these projectiles that come from these weapons you use — these bullets that rip through your organs. Primitive, like our weapons once were—but effective. A bullet can kill you. These asteroids will kill your world. This might destabilize the other planets in your system over a period of years—resulting in a wider tragedy," the Lizardanian motioned to his friend who made an adjustment to the device with what looked something like an old fashioned door key, but with fewer angles. The image of the Twins hitting the planet was displayed…as were the results. The room was absolutely silent. It was the most horrifying thing I've ever seen. The world just folded in on the holes made by the huge rocks, and they flew out the other end. It was awful; I hate to think of it. It was like…old fruit when it gets squished or maybe hit with a B-B gun. The screen went dark and then reappeared with the Twins back at their original, scaled distance. Everyone sighed; people were sweating, breathing hard.

"Our plan is to establish a line just beyond your moon. From this line, we will pour all our power into the asteroids with the intent of splitting them in half before they reach our inner defense positions, then firing at the four resultant pieces until they are small enough to be burned in your atmosphere. Your atomic weapons I will discuss in a moment. The pollution you have created in your atmosphere has thinned your natural defenses against these kinds of events, which doesn't help," Littorian sounded scolding in his last observation and eyed the well-heeled assembly who fidgeted in embarrassment. And fidget they should have, too.

As the Lizardanian lord spoke, the three dimensional event he described unfolded as massive laser-like beams projecting from the Lizardanian crafts, splitting the comets in a fireball of heat, sparks and splintering metal, rock and ice.

"You see," instructed Littorian, now actually using a wooden pointer he'd spied upon entering the conference room to stab into the images cast before the group, "the Twins are more metal than rock, the metal of planet cores, very dense, though not near, thank the Galaxies, the density of collapsed stars, of course."

The Lizardanian regarded his nervous audience thoughtfully. Waves of understanding and knowledge were flowing from Littorian to me. I tried to give back.

"Your nuclear weapons, made more destructive, won't be enough. If only we had the Parcharia now, our work on your weapons could proceed more quickly—they know more about such things! We can't count on the success of Katrina, for they may elect not to fight for you. They admire her and if anyone could convince them to commit to your salvation, it would be Katrina. You noticed how they cleaned the rivers and the lakes of Russia as a tribute to her before they left? This I see as an encouraging sign."

I struggled to hide my surprise. I was still unconscious in the Saint Albans hospital when that gift was given.

"We will launch your weapons at the Twins at this point," with that the screen flashed and the lights of the conference room fell dark—the strange sounds of space filled the room. Without air through which sound moves, how was this possible? The sounds, nevertheless, of warfare against the Twins positively shook the Tank's walls. Dynamic images of the Earth and the moon and the Twins presented themselves in mid-air. A long line of missiles — in four waves launched from several positions — flew toward the four sections of jagged asteroid. The first group of missiles detonated not on impact, but somewhat in front of their targets in blinding flashes, debris scattering everywhere across space.

"This is the result of your weapons after we have channeled their nuclear energy to project inward at the core of the asteroid halves. Surface blasts will not do, in our estimation. We have also invited you to gather as much of your nuclear waste as you wish, to be rid of it. We are now making corebonds — containers — for this waste. Ridding yourselves of your radioactive materials like the rather primitive and actually dangerous enriched uranium you use would make this a safer world, should it survive. We can show you, if Lizardania so decides and the time in fact comes, how to make your nuclear energy usage far cleaner and safer," the Lizardanian sounded a little patronizing to me, but I knew he meant well. At this, the Lizardanian reached down to the pitcher of water that had been placed by the podium from which he towered over the group. He threw back his huge head and opened his massive jaws, emptying the entire contents into a cavernous throat without a drop slipped. Littorian returned the spent container to the conference table.

Immediately, aids rushed forward, an Air Force lieutenant and an Army staff sergeant, and replaced the empty pitcher with two full ones exactly like the first. The Lizardanian gestured appreciation and looked after the water boys with curiosity as they resumed their places standing in the back of the room. It reminded me of ball fetchers at Wimpliton.

"Alligatorian cruisers and our other friends will form the last line of defense, firing on the large remaining sections of the Twins of Triton. Smaller pieces will still penetrate your atmosphere and could do tremendous damage, particularly if they hit large bodies of water at real speed. These reduced pieces will vary in size from 50 to 200 yards across, possibly bigger, and must be destroyed in the inner atmosphere. Your planet's Air Forces are being modified now to assist us in destroying these asteroid pieces. We will modify your missiles to implode their targets, using the density of the material against it," at that the Lizardanian reached down and proceeded to drain another pitcher, plunking it down with some satisfaction. It was promptly replaced by two new pitchers of ice water by the same dutiful team. This brought a slight chuckle to the room and a saber tooth grin from Littorian.

"Finally, at the points of impact that we would expect to see the most dangerous pieces of asteroid, our teams are working with your engineers to modify your missile systems. Along side them will be Lizardanian, Alligatorian, Orcharia and Sereeian laser weapons to target those section of asteroid that evade everyone else. I am very impressed with these laser towers," a picture of the world filled the screen with glowing dots indicating positions of anti-comet batteries. "They are magnificent. But they must be removed if we succeed, for the obvious reasons."

General Yahzov, General Krahotkin and Katrina's father sat in the audience and laughed with everyone else as the Lizardanian then pitched back one container of water after the other, draining them all in a few seconds, to the exasperation of the lieutenant and his assistant standing by a now empty water cooler.

"Well, that's the plan!" Littorian said, slamming down the last empty pitcher with a snort. I half expected dragon fire from his nostrils. The Lizardanian then actually yawned, widely and deeply, revealing row upon backed-up row of long, pointed and perfectly white teeth.

"I have not slept in some time. Unlike Brian, I need my sleep to be an effective strategist. Brian will consult with me while I return to *Tiperia*, the Starfinder. Of this type of Starfinder, only two have attached themselves to our people. *Tiperia* will fight for you, the other stands guard over my homeworld. I will return here in six hours and I expect much progress from everyone by then. Please follow our people's advice, without hesitation," he then turned to me.

"Ready to leave?"

The prospect of visiting a Lizardanian starship had immediate, overwhelming appeal. The thought possessed me and I could now think of nothing else. To step aboard a "Starfinder," talk about TMI!

II

"I have to confess that I've never seen people cooperating like this on anything, even when there are disasters. It seems like only a few people did all the helping when really bad things happen around our world, sometimes our countries don't help one another," as soon as I finished saying it, I regretted doing so. It wouldn't do to let Lizardanians see the worse side of humanity, it occurred to me too late.

"That's curious. You don't share everything in common?" The Lizardanian was directing his vehicle away from the Pentagon below. It served all purposes, it seemed to me, car and inter-atmospheric transport toward Littorian's great flagship, hovering about 60,000 feet in the sky, above the border of West Virginia and Maryland.

"No, I guess not as much as we should," I admitted, now reluctantly.

"If your world doesn't survive...will you come with me to mine?"

I looked down through the clouds to the cities and homes, farms and blue, twinkling lakes. A careful answer was required. I feared offending or upsetting the Lizardanian though this one had given no sign of being easily offended or to be any less than as good as his word. This was an exceptionally noble, chivalrous people, and lying to them, even to put us in a better light, was hard to do. That's how it seemed to me. Changing from Lizardanian to *Universalian*, I said,

"I'd like to...very much...but I would prefer to...die with my people, with my world, if it gets to that."

Littorian made a quick movement and the ship stopped in the air. I warned myself to be careful — a kid burns fast, struck by dragon fire.

The Lizardanian then said, "You're too young to talk so casually about dying. But maybe this is a trait of the human teenager? I won't make you go, though I would be more than disappointed to see you parish just as I'm getting to know you," the creature sighed, as he did from time to time, making him seem...rather human, despite his dragon-like appearance.

I didn't say anything.

"You seem devoted to your kind even if it means your own destruction. For you and the Thirty, there is a way out."

"I'd only let you down...if I let you see me walk away from my world," said I, looking back out for another glimpse of my endangered planet. "You expect more from me."

"What if I offer to take your mother, father, all your family out of danger—would you go with us then if things take a turn for the worse? Think that your family would not have to die with your world. Doesn't that prospect have any appeal for you?" We had now landed within a very large cargo bay, filled with ships of varying dimensions. The place was bedlam, with what looked like a large number of androids and robots working alongside Lizardanians and other aliens at a frantic pace—preparing for battle against the Twins.

"Well...I mean, respectfully...no, my Lord of the Lizardanians."

"You leave me no choice," said he, getting out. My door opened also, and I stepped onto the strangely soft Lizardanian metal. It felt like stepping on sand near the ocean, when it is somewhat hard, saturated with water, yet smooth and inviting. My Lizardanians boots, made of a leather-like material, felt especially adapt at strolling on just this kind of surface.

"No choice?" said I, summoning all my courage.

"We'll just have to save this world, as I said."

"Great. That's cool. What first?"

"A few hours of sleep."

"Now?!"

"Without rest, you won't be at your best and neither will I…we must be prepared to be even more tested than we anticipate. That demands we be rested."

"I worry I'll wake up and you'll have taken me away," I felt unspeakably sad in showing I didn't trust him.

Littorian knelt down before me in the midst of the preparations about us. I looked Littorian in his wonderful double-irised eyes, the blues and greens a hypnotizing and wild mixture. I have never seen the like — their eyes are their most amazing part of their amazing selves.

"I won't let you or your world die without a struggle. I thought that Larascena had killed you before. My heart was broken, for even then I was fond of you — and Katrina. At the time I thought what you'd done to be foolish…only later did I see that it was brilliant. You took the only road that could have to bring you to me on *Tiperia*. It was a hard road, too hard on you. I didn't know you then. I would not have allowed such a fight if I had. Your plan was reckless — what made you think it would work? You hadn't even thought it through." The Lizardanian rose. Together, he and I walked through the high walled corridors of *Tiperia*. It was an enchanting place, more wonderful than I could have imagined. It was not a sterile, colorless series of corridors, but hallways full of motion, somehow actually *in* motion, undulating like fields of wheat in the Midwest.

"This ship is…alive, isn't it?

The Lizardanian was silent for a moment as we strolled over the rhythmically moving floor.

"By both our world's definitions of 'alive' I believe the answer is yes. But of that, later. Now tell me what you were thinking about concerning Larascena!" Littorian seemed intensely curious, and was on to my tactic of changing subjects. Hands clasped behind his back, Littorian peered over at me as we walked leisurely through *Tiperia's* strange passageways. The walls now reminded me more of blood vessels than hallways, pulsing with a rhythm that could only be that of life.

"I gambled on your...um...*humanity*," I told him, very simply and sincerely, looking into the deep green-blue eyes above me, into the strange glowing cerulean ring about the irises.

The Lizardanian threw back his scaled head and bellowed with laughter, causing passers-by to smile (the aliens) and to stare (the androids and robots, or the "Helpers," as he called them).

"Well that's just CRAZY!" said Littorian in *Universalian* to be sure he was understood.

"Was it? You're here and trying to save us now, right?"

"True, true," conceded Littorian, dropping his head as we strode to the Lizardanian's chambers. Here and there he stopped one of the bustling crew, whether Helpers, aliens or Lizardanians, to ask questions or give advice—he did not seem to give any orders, not to anyone or anything. Everything was framed in the form of polite suggestions always asking if the listener had a better idea about how to pursue this or that.

"You don't tell anybody what to do."

"Your asking me or telling me?" said the Lizardanian in his best English.

"Oh, asking, always asking."

179

"They know better than I what to do. Each Lizardanian is always free to choose his or her own course. We have no leaders, except in odd times like these, and even then, I have no real authority over anyone. I am only recognized as the most powerful of my race, this being just a figurehead role. And the measure of power is not significant, more a technicality than anything else. Maybe like having one more tail feather for certain kinds of birds. Only when great cooperation is required am I thrust into this position — one I don't covet. The respect I get from my people is all I have to motivate them. I have no power, that is, ability to inflict pain, on anyone of them. Nor would I want such," he sniffed heavily, as though disgusted with the thought.

"This ship, for instance, it obeys Lizardanian will at its own discretion," went on Littorian, looked down at my surprise. "Hmmm…apparently, that might be a little hard for you to understand. It is as alive as you or I, as anything in your great oceans that you poison every day, as anything that flies in your polluted skies. You must look again at the things you define as not living, I think, or not thinking, but there is no time to discuss this now."

"Wow — it's tough to comprehend a living starship," said I looking around. "You mean they're like the swords and weapons that Katrina and I used, right?"

"This is a Starfinder. That's what we term them. And the swords that were used on you are also alive, yes. You're lucky to be here."

"Sorry about all that. Really."

"Time moves differently for the Starfinder. We can build starships — but not like these. They care for us, as we for them. But they are not pets, they are partners. We give to each other according to our natures. Their nature is to explore. You performed your music not just for us, but for this Starfinder, too. She is willing to expend her power as a gesture to you and it is in her nature to do so."

"She and her?"

"Yes."

"Sweet," said I in Lizardanian.

"You just said how pretty a flower looks," said Littorian in *Universalian*.

"How do you mean?" was my reply in the same language.

"Enough for now, we must rest—you certainly need it."

"I can't fight you on that."

"After what you humans did to Larascena, I am reluctant to fight you."

"Oh, please..."

"Perhaps some other time, and then only for amusement," said Littorian misunderstanding me for the third time. He gave a raspy, reptilian-sounding chuckle.

We entered a spacious chamber from one of the side hallways. A kind of mat, that looked like it would fall to the floor were any weight placed upon it, hung above an elliptical floor. In the next room, separated only by a oval kind of doorway, a larger such mat defied gravity.

"We will sleep for four hours."

And with that, the Lizardanian moved swiftly toward the larger mat and threw himself into it, and I was certain that he would crash to the deck. But the mat suspended him with ease.

"You are tired."

"You're asking me or telling me?" said I as I lay
down with trepidation on the smooth, bluish, floating
mat. But a peace and a rest suddenly engulfed my
tired body and mind. I had never known such
freedom, a relaxation completely new and utterly
welcome. From Littorian I heard no reply, for he was
already fast asleep...

CHAPTER THIRTEEN
A Storm of Foes

I

"My people will be destroyed without you. You know that!" I stood before the leader of the Parcharia, a Lizardanian at either side of me.

"I'm here because I need you. Come to Earth and fight with your friends. I'll do anything..."

I wore two swords, each jet black, and was dressed entirely in white, a Lizardanian charm in my hair, holding the wild mess back. My cascading robes had no surer beauty anywhere in the galaxy. Down, down, from great heights, I addressed an entire people, 100 billion of them. I tried not to think about what they felt about little me asking for so much.

"What is Parcharia that we should interfere with nature's choices? Is it not unmatched arrogance to think that we should alter the course of things?" The crystalline people moved with ease in their world which everywhere was degrees of whiteness, all crystalline rock. The course of evolution of a crystalline race that had evolved no differently than any other race—only the crystal rather than the cell had somehow won the race up the evolutionary ladder. But I tried to think only of how badly Brian needed me to win these many hearts.

"My people could lose their lives in this defense. Why should we sacrifice for you?"

"Because your people live to give and to explore and to help others—I saw that when you cleaned my people's waters. Russia thanks you and will show its gratitude if you but let us. Don't lose your investment on us, a people determined to correct our mistakes and shortcomings."

"Your proof of worth is—"

"—Within my heart," interrupted I, without shame or hesitation. "And I give my spirit to all Parcharians, everywhere!"
In saying this, I drew a sword and threw myself and the blade before the Parcharian delegation within the Great Hall. All Parcharia had heard and seen me; how, well, it was beyond me. But I could feel them all watching.

Torrillian watched and supported me as best he could. What could the Parcharia ask of me that I would not deliver? I raised my head at the silence that greeted my prostrate form, there on this crystal white world—a world with air I could somehow breath. I stood.

"If you need me to prove my people's worth by fighting you, then choose your strongest champion and decide all the conditions in your favor. If it's necessary for me to beg," and I sank to my knees again, my white dress cascading and falling with me on the crystalline ground. "Then I beg you. I plead. I demand. I entreat. I ask humbly. I ask in anger. I ask in love. I ask you to forgive our primitive state and look to what ought to be rather than what is. I offer you all I have, all we have, all that has been, all that we can be, all that we may yet be. Please, please fight with your friends who are standing guard over my world now, who are too few, who have risked their own lives for the billions of humans on my world and all the innocent living things that live there. For Earth, I beg it. If the price be just my life, then take it!" I rose. With my last sword, I prayed they would take the handle and make an end of me. The burden that if even one of these people elected not to help, that none would, was nearly more than I could endure.

The leader of the Parcharia, Orosa Centra, stepped forward. The creature, neither male nor female, reached out to me, my Lizardanian escorts standing a respectful distance behind, curious about the Parcharian decision.

Orosa Centra spoke to my mind, in clear *Universalian*.

You, Katrina, can beg nothing of us...

I

"Positions?"

Littorian stood on the forward deck of *Tiperia* and looked to the great screen. It opened before the crew and the human command staff to reveal the space between the asteroids and our gathering defenses. Distances were squashed. It was like standing out in naked space, to be on this deck. Like standing on the eyelid of a giant—all shrunk into something one could take in at a glance. The two towering opponents flying toward us at an incredible rate stole the breath of every onlooker. Eirosa and Chirminian blocked out all light.

On Earth, work to erect the huge laser and missile towers continued at a blistering pace. The work would keep going until the weapons were actually firing. The energy and focus we poured into the defense was immense. The sheltering of my race in the wide area of anticipated asteroid impact was in full swing. Factories once idled by economic decline now hummed. No where was there unemployment. Manufacturers turned their entire energy and attention to building the planetary defenses. With the help of Lizardania, work that would have taken years had been completed. Everyone, human and alien, worked literally until they could give no more.

"The Twins will be met in 20 minutes," announced a young Lizardanian, Urielian. I remembered him from our first meeting in Vermont, on that cold night. It seemed a million years ago. Maybe it was.

"From here we will watch and direct the battle," announced Littorian — but he was looking not at the generals and leaders from Earth that he had invited aboard his ship. He was looking at me. In this last hour, all the pangs from drugs were now purged from my body. I felt released from the heroin.

Standing with Littorian and I was the American President as well as the presidents, generals and admirals, prime ministers and leaders of Earth. I noted that none of the other life forms of the planet were represented. But weren't their lives important, too?

I thought my concerns to Littorian who was not offended.

You represent the under-represented, Brian Miller. I understand that the young on your world must bear the world's burdens...such is your lot. This answer from Littorian seemed harsh, but I accepted it. For every owl in its tree, every blade of grass in its field, every whale in her ocean, I would not let any of them down, not before I gave up my own life.

We two acknowledged the assemblage and turned to regard the open skyline before us, unimpeded by boundaries, a full view of the awesome spectacle of the Twins' fiery approach.

II

"We're prepared all along the primary line, I believe?" Loridian was asking Korillia, the group commander of the Lizardanian fleet. A warrior on those rare occasions when Lizardania needed one, Korillia was their most experienced. That she was female only made an impression on us humans when we heard it, almost incidently. None of the other races thought about gender at all. I remembered her immediately as one of those who met us on Hard'dack Hill, and who silently judged us during our musical debates. She was one of the first to stop that terrible back-turning.

"We may be rethinking a lot more than scientific things, if we get through this," I heard an American generals say to his Russian counterpart.

"We have 14 cruisers and eight battle platforms, as you — three of platforms are ours," Korillia said in *Universalian*, a noticeably female sound to her voice.

She waved her long, clawed fingers in a light gesture before the open screens.

"In my view, we have enough power assembled to split the Twins, though our travel energies will not re-power the weapons for at least a solar week thereafter. Following the expenditure, our ships will be defenseless during that period, which shouldn't prove a problem, of course," Korillia paused and ran a hand over the protruding scales on the crown on her head.

"Then we'll move our ships off and see what the humans can do, since our primary weapons energy will be exhausted."

"Yes, that makes complete sense. Thank you."

Littorian then turned back and ran a claw gently along the bar lining his command podium. This bar looked less like a piece of manufactured support than a capillary within a living body. And of course, it was.

III

Urielian stared in surprise at his monitors. He blinked, but the indications remained, steady and true. He must report it, but could he believe it himself? When he did, it shook me to my foundations, because I knew instantly what it meant. In Lizardanian society, the command structure was flat—all Lizardanians were equal, but in times of battle or planetary challenge a primal caste system received unquestioning recognition.

"My Lord Littorian!"

My friend bristled at the unfamiliar words but forced himself to turn immediately toward the younger Lizardanian at the communications monitors.

"Urielian, my friend, what concerns you so?" Littorian sounded calm to all who heard — except me. I knew the feeling, because I had felt it myself. It didn't matter how many miles of space, or what differences in evolution, the feeling was changeless and had a name. It was *fear*.

"Crocodilians accompany the Twins, my Lord!" said Urielian in *Universalian*, still looking at his instruments, checking and rechecking again.

The deliberate, artless announcement created a great stir among every alien present. A murmuring began. It looked to me like the alien defenders were frozen by a sudden blast of arctic wind, worse than anything in Vermont.

The strange word, now whispered everywhere on the great deck of the Starfinder — 'Crocodilians!' — seemed to change everything.

IV

"Littorian, this is Genotdelian. How are you my old friend?"

The Crocodilian's words were translated into *Universalian* aboard *Tiperia*. Before answering, Littorian asked Urielian to connect the entire defense fleet into the conversation. And we humans heard the exchange, whether huddling in shelters and basements, preparing to take to the skies in our modified fighter planes, working to power up the land defense lasers or standing on the deck of *Tiperia*. Billions of humans wondered at implications of all that was said. I reached out to a nearby railing to keep from falling over. It seemed my hopes had been vaporized, dreams of a life with Lizardania after this event, fading fast. I asked myself if there was any way I could have known, or guessed, to anticipate this moment.

"A peace must exist between our races that I was absent to welcome — this is fine news," came Littorian's calm response. "But what mission is it that finds you so far from Crocodilia, Genotdelian?"

The Crocodilian seemed equal to the impromptu wit of the Lizardanian.

"You're interfering with the natural course of events in this region of space, my friend. Let us be plain — we are creatures of action. You assist a race doomed by evolution, by nature, to extinction. Word reached us of this interference by Lizardania just in time. Fortunately we are here to keep you from your mistake. And so we are escorting Eirosa and Chirminian on their proper course. Our forces meet in combat in minutes at our current speed. Certainly the Alligatorians who have already been defeated in what we understand to have been fair combat with one of the Earthers will leave you rather than face our superior weapons. They are embarrassed enough, I should think; no sense in risking further humiliation by standing in the way of nature's course. The Seree and Orcharia know not to interfere, I trust, or at least I presume they have such wisdom. The Parcharia are not in this system so you have already sacrificed much strength against the Twins — and us. Pass from this place in peace, for we have no quarrel with you over such an insignificant planet in an isolated, primitive system. Certainly these, ah, *humans*, are not worth in their total number the existence of even a single Lizardanian! We have been much time between conflicts. You are a young leader. Ask your people if the humans are worth a war. Allow the Twins their path and nature its course!"

Clear to all who heard, Genotdelian was a powerful and convincing speaker. If humanity had a single heart at the moment of the Crocodilian's words, it skipped a beat now, as we awaited the answer. I could not keep from shaking as I stood on *Tiperia* a few weeks ago just another poor kid living in Vermont, now the last hope of the entire world and all its innocent creatures.

But Littorian wasted no time with a reply.

"Lizardania! We are *indeed* creatures of action! What is your answer?"

Korillia's ship unleashed a double blast of energy plasma from its forward-most weapons. The energy hurdled toward Eirosa. The impact ignited on the surface of the asteroid and sends showers of rock and metal in a wide pattern. A fireball of easily ten miles across ignited across the surface. It was dazzling.

"You have our answer, Genotdelian. A massacre of Crocodilians do you face if you battle us. We have modified the human's defenses and you will feel their sting should you enter their atmosphere. The full power of Lizardania will be behind every blast into your ranks. Your ships are too few against us. Turn back or be responsible personally for many a death of your race with a new war hereafter! If we agree on little else, we have always agreed that this life is precious and it should not be wasted. Gather up your reason and wisdom quickly and reconsider your foolish and futile course!"

"It is your interference with nature that is futile! Crocidilia, answer these vermin!" roared Genotdelian, apparently losing complete control of himself, raging about his bridge. "FIRE, FIRE!"

"SHIELDINGS, SHIELDINGS, EVERY SHIP!" was Littorian's deafening response.

At that, the lead ships of the Crocodilians fired on the Lizardanian line.

Massive energy impacts on the collective defense screens, raised only moments before, shook our armada in a blinding light. *Tiperia* herself shuttered, thousands of lights seemed to flicker — but the Starfinder would not buckle against the powerful impacts. Then the awesome, living ship recovered herself. It seemed to me that raw firepower might favor the other side, as Lizardania needed to empty its united energies at the Twins for Littorian's plan to work. There was little to spare for a fight with the Crocodilian ships and maybe Genotdelian knew it.

Littorian knelt down by me, put both hands on my shoulders. This was the second time I had taken so close a look at his patient eyes, now heavy with cares. I tried to stop shaking, but surely Littorian felt my shutters.

"Brian listen to me, now. What is about to happen is not your fault. Nor is it the fault of any human, anywhere. You're not to blame yourself for the next hours. We fight not just for you but for the safety of the home worlds of all whom you have met. Later you will understand why it is better for us to fight here and now. Retreat will welcome attack on those races. Weakness is the invitation for aggression. If we show it here, there will be no end to bullying — you know something about that, don't you? Sometimes you must turn and face your enemies.

Also, know that we have made more than a promise
to your people through your sacrifice. In many ways,
we're going to ask you to sacrifice now for us. Some
Lizardanians are about to pass from this life that we
now share, so it will seem, and so too, I'm afraid will
many of your race. But we believe that while this
conscious life is sacrosanct, it's not the end of
existence when we leave it. Our bodies are strong—
but temporary—we believe in the spirit within.
When you fought Larascena knowing you couldn't
win, we were one with you. It is what you called on
to rid your body of the chemicals that briefly ruled
you. And it will be that spirit that stands with me
now against what we face together. You're called. If
the calling is indeed random, as you believe, it still
must be answered. How do you answer?" The
Lizardanian had left his communications link open so
that not just his own forces had heard, but so had all
humanity—and so had the advancing enemy.

Realizing how many minds and worlds would be
impacted by my reply, I said simply,

"If we must, we're ready to fight. I would ask the
Crocodilians to consider joining us in destroying the
Twins of Triton, which seems like a pretty natural
thing to do and to everybody's advantage...it could
be the beginning of, you know, the Lizardanians and
the Alligatorians and the Crocodilians getting
together, along with all the others we've met. That I
would say thank you now to the Lizardanians and
their friends for standing with us in this final hour—
you won't be sorry and my race will show its
gratitude.

"And if you Crocodilians choose the way of war
rather than of peace with us," I concluded, "then I
hope we send as many of you as possible *straight to*

hell!" I spoke in *Universalian* and everyone
understood my meaning, particularly the reptilian
races concerned.

My words met complete silence for a moment.
"Heart, they have that," said Heritian, leader of the
fighter crafts, accidentally into the still open
communications stream. It was unfortunately for him
picked up by the Lizardanians and the concession
echoed through the lines of the defenders. I soon
learned that Heritian would penetrate Earth's
atmosphere to destroy those defending against the
Twins, had a personal grudge against one
Lizardanian in particular. And I was surprised to
learn which Lizardanian that was.

"Then bring his back to me, Heritian," said
Genotdelian grimly on the same communications
stream. "And those of as many of the others as you
care to collect."

V

"I think that's quite enough. Close
communication to the Crocodilians, please," added
Littorian. "Ensure that we have maximum security on
all communications hereafter. We need silence for the
obvious tactical reasons," he added.

"It is done, Lord Littorian," said Urielian.

"Thank you. Fleet and Earth defenses, listen
carefully, we must adjust our plan. Lizardanian ships
will fire at the Twins in one minute. After that, our
ships will only be targets, as their weapons energies
will be exhausted. Lizardanians, save what you can
for your defense screens, but we must split the Twins.

Lizardanian ships will then fall back immediately to the planet. The Crocodilians do not know about the human's missiles — this kind of nuclear technology is something they won't expect. While inferior, with our enhancements made, they'll be effective enough in their large numbers. Earth Control, retarget the first line of missiles to explode within the ranks of the Crocodilians as they come between the Moon and the planet. *One section in three,* prepare to meet the Crocodilians, the rest will remain focused on the Twins."

I couldn't conceal a look of respect at the command and strategic thinking ability of my new friend. All the humans respected the wisdom in Littorian's orders with faces aglow in the modulating lights of the Lizardanian craft, all in awe.

"Orcharia and Alligatoria, you will be assigned the dual challenge of engaging both the Crocodilians and the larger asteroid pieces. Earth Air Forces! You will face the fighters of the Crocodilians led by a very powerful Crocodilian, Heritian. It is not you but rather Soreidian who will face this one. Do not engage Heritian if you see him, report his location. Heritian is far beyond any of the rest of you. Leave him to Soreidian. They have a personal score to settle which has nothing to do with any of us. Heritian's ship has five extended wings and is very pale green in color, different from all others. The Crocodilian ship signatures will be fed to your computers and targeting systems. Attack the other Crocodilians only in formation with our people, or you will be overwhelmed.

"Soreidian, are you prepared?"

"I'm leaving now, my Lord Littorian," with that, I caught the eye of the former Mr. Triassic.

Best wishes for your success, Mr. Triassic.

It is exceptionally ironic to me that I should be thanking you now for your thoughts, but I do. I was wrong about you, about you and Katrina! I would take back my words and deeds in the classroom — I did not know you then. You are noble race and much is possible from you.

Thank you for defending my world, Soreidian.

I defend it, but for all of us.

Please be careful and come back to us in one piece.

In this, I will try…

That the Lizardanian was finally thinking kindly to me produced a surge of emotion that I could not hold back. I actually ran forward and embraced Soreidian. Soreidian made a display of embarrassment. But he did not back away and I felt his huge hand rest on my shoulder for a moment.

"Lord Littorian, we are ready to fire," it was Loridian, taking the lead in directing the initial attack on the Twins.

"Expend all your energy, my friend, and get your ships away — land them on the planet and send your people and our Helpers to assist with the ground defenses. They are needed there anyway."

Littorian sounded cool and confident in his "advice," but I could still feel internal doubts, feelings I knew he shared with no one else. The intimacy of this sharing was something I had known only with Katrina. Immediately, the line of Lizardanian craft fired past the lead Crocodilians aiming for the Twins. Crocodilian fighters swarmed in toward the line of Lizardanian ships, firing with inhuman accuracy. Like dolphins defending against sharks, the overlapping shieldings of the Lizardanian ships absorbed blow upon blow, protecting the group. The blinding explosions as the Lizardanians expended themselves on the Twins of Triton was like watching a thousand fireworks displays. The concussions of the particle and energy beam weapons made even the noiselessness of space sounded out in terrific explosions. I felt and heard these even from within *Tiperia's* protection.

The Twins buckled and were actually propelled backward in space, so powerful were the Lizardanian blows. *Tiperia* lead the firing with an energy so powerful that I can't comprehend it, even now. But not four pieces of asteroid resulted from the onslaught, but only three! And Chirminian was apparently harder than anticipated, denser and while greatly reduced, remained in one monstrous piece.

Littorian was awed and stricken, but only for a moment. He'd underestimated the Twins of Triton, but that was now behind him. There was yet time.

"Well done!" roared Littorian in triumph, "your energy for this task is gone, now with all speed return to the planet and let us assist with the defenses there!"

The Lizardanian ships broke formation and turned away from the wounded asteroids. One of the Lizardanian battle platforms were already on fire and seemed to me completely engulfed and encircled by attacking Crocodilian ships. Thick clouds of many colors from the ignited oxygen aboard the Lizardanian ship billowed into space. Escape craft were launched from yet another crippled Lizardanian ship that had already begun to fall into empty space, out of control, the Crocodilian warships committing the atrocity of firing on the escapees without mercy or quarter. I could hardly control my anger. I was now full of the knowledge and gifts of these people, and my pain at seeing them dying was beyond even what Larascena had inflicted. It was worse than the let-down of the heroin when it had fled my bloodstream. Even Larascena was now in the line of Alligatorian defense, was fighting for the survival of Earth. I was so in touch with the defending aliens that I could feel their spirits leaving their broken bodies. I gripped the rail, struggling to stand up. That such noble and beautiful people were dying for little humanity was too much.

I fell to my knees, involuntarily reaching out to the borderless screen before me. I wished I could clasp the hand of but one Lizardanian on the destroyed battle platform and pull him, or her, to safety.

No, don't turn away, Brian, and don't cry for them — they are, and yet remain, Lizardanians. Stand, now. They will be alright, though that may be hard for you to understand today. Allow them to depart nobly for their own and for their beliefs. They fall fighting an old enemy that has nothing to do with humanity. That our two different fights should now overlap is as regrettable as it was, probably...inevitable...

I got up. A lump in my throat and my tears rose again as yet another Lizardanian ship appeared to be in trouble, pursued back to Earth, with two Crocodilian cruisers, firing at the Lizardanian's thrusters. Clearly it could not return fire, having expended all its weapon energy at the Twins.

"Observe Crocodilian tactics," said Littorian grimly. "One day, you will face one of them yourself. I will teach you to fight them — and others — long before. Watch and remember their culture knows no mercy.

"Alligatorians, you will have to focus on Chirminian depending on the success of the human's nuclear weapons," Littorian said toward the great screen.

I felt, in spite of his hopeful words, that Littorian's heart was breaking. To look at him, he appeared the leader of his people, strong, sound, and calm. The human heads of state were amazed at their first encounter with interplanetary warfare. To them, the images were more powerful than any movie or picture from imagination, beyond any dream. I looked over and saw them all staring out of the borderless screen, into the space battle between enemy ships, our allies and the broken Twin sections. Our losses were staggering, but it was going worse for the Crocodilians—and the Twins. The action moved far quicker, in the same way that watching a car accident on the scene has ten times the impact of seeing one in a theatre.

"We are prepared—I could not restrain all the Orcharia to remain in their line. Some have rushed to defend your ships. They search for survivors among whom, you know, we've many dear friends. I am sorry for my inability to maintain line discipline!" it was the leader of the Orcharia, Terraline speaking.

"No blame, Terraline. Thank you for attempting to stand steady. I know the feelings between our people are too strong for orders." Littorian then commanded, not at all suggested, somewhat ahead of schedule, "Launch all waves of the human's missiles!"

A dozen long lines of rockets emerged from launch sites all over our planet. The boosters placed on them by Lizardanian design and much human labor brought them quickly into the battle. The

missiles seemed to take the Crocodilians by surprise.
The Earth emptied itself of its most horrific weapons.
I watched them speeding to toward the Twins.
Designed to kill humanity, they were now about to
help save it.

The Crocodilians had been preoccupied with long
range firing on the Alligatorian and Orcharia
defenses. The missiles, a strange site to them, were at
first thought to be a line of engaging fighter craft. But
the confusion did not last long.

"Shoot those craft down, shoot them all down
now, they aren't ships, they can't maneuver!" it was
Heritian yelling into his voice unit. "They target the
Twins, they must be destroyed!" We had picked up
Heritian on an open channel, his angry voice captured
and delivered to us by the perceptive Urielian.

A wild change of course on the part of the
Crocodilians ships began, as they fired at our rockets
and were in turn the blasted by the Orcharia and
Alligatorians. Some of the missiles were destroyed,
and quickly. But intense fire from the allied craft
protected the lion's share.

The nuclear weapons exploded in successive
waves, the first line detonated on or near the surface
of Chirminian, splitting the asteroid into not two but
three sections, and further reducing the huge swaths
of Eirosa. And yet, massive sections of asteroid were
still falling toward the planet, not significantly altered
from their initial course.

"Ground defenses and Earth Air Forces,
prepare!" Littorian's voice was full of the loudness of
war. The Crocodilians continued their relentless
attack, a lengthy line of their fighter craft now
heading down into the atmosphere.

The human generals were in touch with their forces, the ability to recognize the difference between friend and foe in the skies successfully communicated into every weapons control system.

"It's time for me to go," Soreidian said and Littorian nodded his approval. My old teacher left the group of Lizardanians coordinating defenses and headed toward his personal fighter.

"Please be careful," was the last thing I told him. I couldn't believe I once hated him.

"Hey, no worries, man," smiled Soreidian and he was gone.

After a time, we heard these words. "Littorian, I would speak with you,"

It was Genotdelian again on a different communication wavelength from the one that had been terminated earlier. Littorian glanced with annoyance at Urielian. I had not seen this look of agitation from my friend. It was frightening enough. The younger Lizardanian at communications looked perplexed, apparently unaware that such a communication was now possible. Horrible sounds of interplanetary battle resounded around us, the sounds of metallic ripping, energy weapons firing, the eerie noise of laser strikes inflicted on the flesh of *Tiperia* and continuous booming and echoing from blast impacts.

"I listen, Genotdelian, but with sadness that so many of your people have already been destroyed. Your fleet was not prepared for our defenses, and more surprises await you beyond the destruction caused by the human's nuclear technology — apparently you didn't anticipate that either. What do you want?"

"Direct your attention to the planet's moon and

you'll have my answer. That is a suitable response, I suspect, to your arrogance and your foolish decision to stand in nature's path," said Genotdelian.

Nearly as large a Crocodilian fleet as that already engaged was hastening from the moon's direction. It quickly took an organizing pattern, and massed into an attack formation. The lines of new enemy ships were very long. They were in very close formation, wings almost overlapping, at rows six deep.

"Gather your survivors and leave the Earthers to their fate! You have killed many more of my people than I have of yours, but our readings here show that we have already exterminated half the Lizardanians in this system. That makes you responsible for the extinction of one in four of your entire race! And we have lost count of the humans in their worthless airplanes that we have crushed into oblivion. That primitive and weak race is forfeit. We now engage your towers on the surface. Soon they will all be destroyed. Take your Thirty with you now—yes, we know about them and a good deal more about what you've done, too. I know the consequence of your act—and face the wrath of your people for your foolishness." Genotdelian said it all thickly and slowly.

Littorian looked perplexed. He did the math with me, and we didn't like the result. Even after his calculation was run mentally between us ten times with ten different scenarios, we both got the same answer. Each resulted in disaster.

Littorian looked down from the podium at the humans below. He glanced toward the representatives of the allies of Lizardania, standing near, whose allegiances went deeper than blood. I heard his internal thoughts. Had he taken us all too far? Could he be blamed now for carrying on a fight that no one had anticipated? How could the Earth defenses engage both the Crocodilian's new fleet and fire at the still planet-killing potential of asteroid sections hurdling down, the largest of which had escorts of many Crocodilian ships? What would the galaxy think of a Lizardanian defeat? All these thoughts consumed the young leader. I tried to help him think, but I was also out of ideas. He turned back and silently stared at the long rows of advancing Crocodilian ships. Every human general could feel the burden on the Lord of Lizardania. Some of them knew what it was like, all what it must be like, to encounter insane odds. If placed in the identical position, they knew the inevitable command that must be given. The generals lowered their heads. Clear to me, it was all over.

Finally Littorian looked at me.

"Save your own people," I said to him in Lizardanian, relieving my friend of the great pressure of a Lizardanian promise over foolish suicide. "You've done all that could be done, and more — let us fight it out now alone. Please bring me and the other humans quickly home, and then…just go." It was not as hard for me to say as I'd thought. It eased my mind to know that I could save some of allies now defending my world.

My friend said nothing.

Littorian looked then from me to his own people. Resignation was to be read on every Lizardanian face, too. There could be no more point in fighting — all that was left was the prospect of a broken world, defeated allies and a general massacre.

Littorian appeared angry for a moment, his prodigious personal strength frustrated by the situation. Then he sighed heavily, at which motion the humans below knew too what my advice had been, even though the Lizardanian language remained a mystery to them.

"We can't ask the kid for anything else, sir," whispered Presidential Advisor Mike French. The President nodded, looked to his generals and the other world leaders. There was nothing left to say.

"Genotdelian," said Littorian very slowly, staring at the new Crocodilian attackers near the moon. The allied ships were reforming their lines, as though they intended to charge their numerically superior enemy. Their heroism was something to behold. And I was glad my friend wouldn't order them now to charge futility, to their deaths. And yet they were preparing to advance, regardless of the futility. I saw the reorganized line was lead by none other than Larascena! I was glad she would live through this day when I took back the Lizardanian's promise.

"I listen to you, as they say, *Lord of the Lizardanians*? That's what they call you at a time like this?" said Genotdelian in self-satisfied mockery. "What a ridiculous little title."

"Genotdelian...let me now ask...about terms for—" Littorian stopped and looked again toward the moon. "—your immediate and unconditional *surrender!*" The Lizardanian was grinning broadly. Shocked, everybody looked from Littorian to the gathered Crocodilian ships.

The Parcharia fleet had arrived! They were already engaging the Crocodilians with abandon, their massive warships cutting through the new Crocodilian line, weapons alight with a terrible accuracy. Extended between many, many of the Parcharian ships were huge golden nets, with intricate energy lacing. These ships threw themselves into the Crocodilian formation, and gathered ships up like fishermen taking in their catch. The nets shoved the enemy ships against one another, resulting in huge explosions and total chaos within the ranks of the Crocodilians. I couldn't count the number of enemy craft scattered and destroyed. They fought back, but now Larascena's reformed line was firing on the Crocodilians, too. It was horrible, and at once glorious. My hate for war was boundless, but so now was my joy.

Explosions rippled through the Crocodilian ships, arrayed so closely together in their attack formation that damaged ships slammed one into another, magnifying the destruction among the unsuspecting enemy. More nets came from the flanks and a rout began to take shape. The surprise brought by the Parcharians was complete, and so was the disarray among the enemy. Half of the remaining Orcharia and Alligatorian ships immediately broke orbit to support the Parcharia, joining Larascena's line of defenders, the other half valiantly redoubled their efforts against the remains of the Twins.

There came then a voice came over the usual communications band reserved for Lizardanian transmissions, a very human, Russian voice...

VI

"You didn't think I'd let you get all the credit, did you, Brian?" It was Katrina, with her usual brashness.

"Kat! I knew you'd do it!"

The bridge of *Tiperia* became a mad house of celebration and excitement. The generals and the other humans hugged their alien counterparts, grappling hands joyously with the surprised Lizardanians, as the battle ragged on.

"You had no such foreknowledge," she snapped. "And there's a lot to do yet — I hope Littorian will tell me you've done something of use while we've been gone."

"This one has certainly done her share, Lord Littorian," said Torrillian, then. "I will join Soreidian and the rest of our people now, with your blessing."

Littorian said, "You have it and welcome. Thank you for...for...sparing me..." he didn't finish. He was not yet recovered from his near-decision to sacrifice billions at the signaling of retreat. He shuttered.

Command does NOT suit me, he thought to me, then and there.

"But I don't know where Soreidian is at the moment. Urielian, any sign of him?"

"We were tracking his ship over an area known as the Black Sea — he was engaging Heritian — now both ships have moved out of contact."

VII

Allied starships continued to battle both asteroid and Crocodilian, Katrina saving the day.

Meanwhile, Soreidian had found a pale green ship while the Earth Air Forces carried on a valiant defense of the inner atmosphere. The humans were losing fighters at a rate of twenty to one. Their planes were armed with Lizardanian weapons but were too slow, despite modifications, to engage the Crocodilians. Heritian had personally destroyed dozens of human planes before Soreidian found him.

The ground crews supported were they could. But their main targets, in a sky filled with them, were the largest asteroid pieces that had defied the Earth's protective atmosphere. Individual fighter pilots began to make the terrible choice — their lives for the planet. The horrible spectacle of jets ramming directly into Crocodilian ships was repeated over and over, comrades wishing each other well in teary, courageous, and final transmissions. Though many were blasted from the skies before their kamikaze missions were completed, a heavy toll was taken on the Crocodilians. They were confounded at the insane tactic, one beyond their understanding. But neither was the existence of their race hanging in the balance.

The skies were alight with laser exchanges, rockets intended to destroy asteroid sections, fireballs of ships impacted by exploding particles of the Twins, energy blasts from the huge ground towers firing upward or from the star cruisers dropping into the atmosphere to engage in the battle. Again and again, the Earth air force pilots guided their planes into the enemy ranks, a macabre display of burning self-sacrifice.

On the quickening pace of the destruction of his combined fleets, Genotdelian gazed in amazement, surprise, unspeakable hatred and disgust.

Clearly it was time to withdrawal — the Parcharia had tipped the balance.

Parcharia, you will pay for this, make no mistake!

Genotdelian thought toward the Parcharian flag ship, intending his thought to reach Orosa Centra himself. There was no response, though Genotdelian recognized his counterpart's command ship directing the Parcharian fleet.

The Parcharian cruisers and battle platforms were remarkably effective and seemed to defy counterattack. Withdraw was the only hope for the Crocodilians since the Twins were now but shadows; their destructive power halved, then quartered, and now quartered again, capable of less and less destruction as the moments past. The humans and their allies fought with a self-sacrificing courage that grudgingly impressed the Crocodilian leaders. The humans appeared indifferent to the wounds and death they received themselves, bent completely on the salvation of their world. Half the human planes were already destroyed, yet the remainder fought on, ramming themselves into Crocodilian craft, great and small, having given up on trying to blast through the enemy's shielding. Genotdelian quietly ordered the withdrawl and turned his flagship toward home. He watched *Tiperia* only a few miles away.

The attack command ship followed Genotdelian's in the retreat.

"Tercharian!"

"I am here Regent. My ship is badly damaged and my command is all but destroyed!"

"I don't care about any of that!" roared Genotdelian leaping from his command chair. "Now, listen carefully. You have some of the old planet bombs aboard your ship, do you not, as command lead?"

"Yes, yes...we have two, as you know. But they are only for self-destruction of the fleet."

"Put them into your launch bays, with proximity-to-planet fuses. Launch them at the planet — pay attention now! Fire them on my order, one at a time. Communications, open a stream to *Tiperia*."

"They do not respond, my Regent."

"Helm, bring us about and fire on *Tiperia* the moment she is in close-contact range. They'll respond to that!"

"Thirty seconds to range, Regent."

VIII

Urielian interrupted our celebration aboard *Tiperia*.

"Lord Littorian! Genotdelian is turning to engage us!"

I whirled around from the happy faces of my own people.

Littorian leapt from the gathering of well-wishers and back to the command rostrum. I flew to his side.

"Weapons status? Defense shieldings?"

"All but exhausted! We have power to maintain orbit only, my lord. Worse, a weapon has just been launched toward the planet!"

I saw a faint vapor trail escape the Crocodilian command ship. As it did, Genotdelian swung his own cruiser around to get into attack range. The vapor trail was heading toward North America.

Littorian was equal to the moment.

"Convert orbital power to forward energy beams, target-up that device! Fire!"

Tiperia discharged a bolt of blue and orange light even before Littorian had finished speaking. A flickering began throughout *Tiperia* and ship momentarily went dark. When light returned, it was very dim. A concussion from the resulting massive explosion rocked the Starfinder.

"Losing altitude, my lord. Now losing life supporting systems." But almost immediately, a second vapor trail sped from the command ship. As it did, Genotdelian's ship hurried to complete its turn. I saw the intent now of the two enemy ships. Once again, *Tiperia* fired true and destroyed the planet bomb as it entered the Earth's outer atmosphere. But this time the light did not return to *Tiperia's* deck. The ship was exhausted, I could feel she was fully drained and the ship was listing hard. She was only strong enough to preserve herself and those of us aboard her. She was intent on landing on the surface, she couldn't sustain our life supporting systems, and we continued to rapidly descend toward the vast ocean of the Pacific. In the complete darkness, we watched helplessly as Genotdelian's ship completed its turn to face us, we without power for defenses or weapons, he matching our free fall speed.

Then light from within the ship appeared, near Littorian and I, at the command rostrum.

Time seemed to stop.

Genotdelian's ship, as it turned on us, seemed to halt its motion. Before us, a shape appeared and solidified, all in white, enshrouded in a long, hooded cloak gathered around a kneeling creature. We could see none of its features. Its garment covered it and the hood formed a depression within which none of us could see.

Still time remained stopped.

Who is this? I thought to Littorian.

It is Tiperia, was the calm answer.

Everyone was silent, as a silken hand moved aside the hood and a face looked out to us. It was a very young woman — only to me and the other humans. To the others, it looked like a young Lizardanian female, or an Alligatorian or whatever race beheld it — but always a female of any given species.

Littorian approached the kneeling figure. It rose, and not quickly. It was very tall, even taller than a Lizardanian. When I heard the voice, it was of a woman, certainly, one infinitely kind, patient and very tired.

"My friend Tiperia," said Littorian.

The robed figure turned to regard the Lizardanian. And it smiled in a disarming way.

"My friend Littorian," said Tiperia. And there was mirth in the voice, all contentment and calm, a loving voice.

"Tiperia, are you much injured?"

"I am not. I am only tired."

"You have saved your cousin."

"The humans have caused her pain."

"The Twins would have killed her."

"These humans may yet."

"They may yet learn."

"You will see to it?"

"I can try, Starfinder."

"I should like that."

"Death may come."

"He is no end."

"Not for you."

"Not for us. Behold…"

At that instant, when the Universalian exchange between Littorian and Tiperia ended, Genotdelian's ship unloaded. A withering display of blues, greens, yellows and whites, the destructive energy plasmas tearing simultaneously across the short distance — I shut my eyes, turning my face into the cloak of Littorian. A great burst from the resultant explosions hid *Tiperia* from view, masked her in a wide, arching energy field.

The blast screens across Genotdelian's view would have kept him from seeing his victory. When he could see again, moments later, he certainly expected to see only pieces of Starfinder debris. Instead *Tiperia* was still there, untouched by his efforts, yet not free from damage, and still descending gently to Earth.

From under and behind *Tiperia*, four Parcharians battle platforms came into view, having protected *Tiperia* with their long-range shielding. Each now fired upon and pursued Genotdelian's ship.

Orcharia ships also arrived seconds later to fire on Genotdelian's retreating armada. They inflicted heavy damage and destroyed many of the smaller Crocodilian attack craft whose ranks had already been savaged by the sacrificing men and women of the Earth Air Forces and their new friends.

Genotdelian was certainly looking upon his once proud line of ships with anger in the extreme. I knew he, and not my friend, would have explaining to do once he arrived home. He deserved whatever he got — as long as it was bad.

IX

I learned what befell Soreidian and told it to Katrina. The two were engaged in single combat, low in Earth's atmosphere. Above them, Crocodilian ships were breaking out of orbit, in a despairing retreat.

The two ships continued to exchange fire. Both the Lizardanian and Heritian's fighter craft were hopelessly damaged and near breaking up—their ability to turn and fire while holding position in the air had been devastating to both. They flew over the Bering Sea; Soreidian chasing Heritian, each craft exchanged energy blasts with brutal accuracy, losing power and their ability to stay aloft.

"I hear your people are in retreat, Heritian. I will allow you to run away, if you wish," Soreidian told his old foe.

"Soreidian, I told you once that I'd kill you myself and without weapons—I'll see you at the grid location I'm transmitting now. If you're not a coward, you'll be there. And I will rip you to pieces. You should hurry, for if I meet any more humans like the ones I've already killed in these skies they will suffer a similar fate," at that the Crocodilian craft fell like any anvil directly toward the open plains of Russia. Soreidian, hardly needed the threat to encourage him, followed. Had I been focused on this event, I would have insisted that the former Mr. Triassic have some major back-up.

X

Brian let me, Katrina, tell of Sordiean's story.

In a small Russian town, two smoldering and sparkling spacecraft landed heavily in Alexander Ivanov Kamenev's "second best" wheat field. The field was blanketed by snow. Every few feet held stubborn stalks refusing to surrender to winter. Several neglected pieces of farm equipment waited in the snow for their owner's commands. The small hamlet had been told that huddling in basements in their location was unnecessary, so they were gathered instead around the few television sets and radios in town.

A child noticed the smaller war; all the other villagers enthralled by coverage of battle against Twins and now, it appeared, against a rival group of reptilians. Deaths were listed in the hundreds rather than the tens of millions. The Earth's Air Forces were performing miracles, but at a great cost. The Twins were being defeated and the enemies of Lizardania, the Crocodilians, were in full retreat. The bursting sounds of joy completely drown out the little girl's chirping.

"Mama! Papa! Two of the Star Dragons are fighting at Kamenev's! Come and see!"

The village heeded the youngster with dread and fear, and rose as one person, walking out to the field. They approached cautiously as the two huge creatures engaged in hand-to-hand struggle, no weapons to be seen, wrestling in the snow. Aware of what destruction such creatures could deliver, the villagers gathered what weapons came to hand, mainly farm implements. There were very few guns. Had I been there, I would have told them how useless bullets were.

"This will hurt—but you won't live to feel the pain," Heritian hissed in *Universalian*.

The two reptilians fought with powerful blows and swipes of their long claws. They dug in with their massive teeth, always seeking to rip beneath the scales. It was a battle befitting, perhaps, that very patch of ground some 200 million years before when great dinosaurs fought for flesh and territory.

Seconds became minutes and the minutes became twenty, the two exchanging punches and lashes of incredible force. From beneath the scales, blood was forced to yield, Soreidian's a thick bluish purple, the Crocodilian's a more watery, dark green-blue. With every miss of a tail, the ground shook as if convulsed by a small earthquake. And upon a connection, those watching could feel the concussion, shockwaves that ran completely through their frightened bodies. Anyone would be transfixed, as I've since seen such fights.

Heritian managed a series of smashing, unanswered blows and sent Soreidian to the ground.

"Time to die, Lizardanian."

But as the Crocodilian prepared to tear into Soreidian's heaving back, a tremendous report sounded and sparks burst across Heritian's chest, backing the creature up a pace from his foe. Unharmed by the blast, Heritian looked bewildered — but only for a moment.

Mr. Kamenev stood in a cloud of blue smoke, some distance from the knot of villagers. He had retrieved his old shotgun and emptied both barrels at Heritian. Startled and then realizing, the Crocodilian immediately walked briskly toward the solitary human. In considerable pain, but not from the shotgun pellets, he decided Soreidian would be on the ground long enough to dispense with this Russian fool.

The rest of the villagers watched helplessly as the huge Crocodilian narrowed the distance between himself and the old man with long strides. Instead of running, the elderly farmer simply reloaded calmly and took aim once again.

BBBLLLAAAMMM!!!

Another perfect shot. But Heritian was prepared for the minor impact and his stride did not shorten in the least. Mr. Kamenev brought down the barrels, emptied the tubes of their spent cartridges and prepared to reload. But by then, Heritian was standing before him. The village gasped as the creature raised a hand of claws and brought it sweeping down.

The weapon splintered and scattered across the snow, like any pastic toy. The shocked farmer watched as the hand was brought up a second time, then downward with a great swishing of sliced air.

Another set of claws met those intended for Mr. Kamenev's throat as Soreidian hurdled his full weight into Heritian, the two combatants again rolling over in the snow. The teeth were locked together, and though they looked like ivory, the clashing sounded like steel against steel.

Mr. Kamenev blinked and then observed the blasted pieces of his favorite weapon. It was quite beyond repair, all splintered wood and sliced metal.

Soreidian gained the upper hand on his foe. But Heritian would not yield, and kept ferociously at the wounds he'd given Soreidian already. The Lizardanian felt himself being bled away, and summoned himself for a last, titanic effort. There were no signs of a rescue party. It was clear the humans could be of no real assistance. Soreidian ignored Heritian's teeth locked around his right leg and, with his jaws open to their full extent, brought his teeth together around Heritian's head. The

Lizardanian's long, great incisors bore down like a vice against a rock. The rock was cracking.

Finally, a very loud report like a third blast from old Kamenev's gun sounded, but even louder, causing the villagers to leap back. Heritian slid from Soreidian's teeth in a pool of dark blue mess, finished, the Crocodilian's entire skull crushed in. The amount of incredible strength required for such a result is bewildering to contemplate for me, even now. The snow was a bizarre pattern of white, green-blue, and purple, pierced by golden wheat shafts.

The Lizardanian stood, reached out to the open air to steady himself, bleeding heavily from a dozen wounds. He staggered about his enemy, for a moment unconvinced of Heritian's end, then fell over into the snow and stalks. The villagers moved forward with caution and observed the scene in whispers, pointing, the hands grasping their tools as weapons.

Soreidian was nearly too weak even to speak.

When he did, he could only think of English words he'd learned as a teacher in class with Brian and me. He found himself regretting learning Russian. And now, bleeding steadily from his many open wounds, he was afraid. It was an emotion he had only known a few times in his long life. The farm tools could find his hurts. And there were very many people around him now, probably too many to kill in his weakened condition. He had never felt so tired, so vulnerable. He recalled Brian's words that night a milieu ago in the Pentagon,

I hate you for what you're doing – to my people – and I know you'll be paid out for this crime – soon, too!

The villagers stood over Soreidian. They recognized the victor as one of those fighting for the defense of the planet, and considered the creature's rescue of Mr. Kamenev.

"We know who you are, Mr. Star Dragon, and we're going to help you," one of the villagers said in Russian. Soreidian stared back and said that he needed help in *Universalian*, but he couldn't be certain that the villagers would know what to do.

Soreidian was totally drained. Had he known the cost in facing Heritian, he admitted to me later, he would not have done it. He lay there, wondering how long it would be before a search party found him—and whether he would be alive to greet them.

The people moved forward. Flashed before Soreidian were his deeds done to Brian and me. Could they not recognize him as one of the tormentors of the pair during the musical Presentations? Soreidian had never known a helpless moment until today, there in Mr. Kamenev's snowy, "second best" wheat field.

Many hands reached out. He shivered at their touch, wondering if some deeper, cosmic justice was about to be done.

The villagers attempted to lift him. Even with twelve men trying, they could not pick up the Lizardanian for more than a few seconds. Old Kamenev had been watching the attempt some yards away, his old brows furrowed. He was still in anguish over the loss of his precious shotgun. He'd never known the like—and he strode briskly away.

The villagers again attempted to lift Soreidian and carry him back to the village, but they dropped him, evoking a growl that frightened several of them. Soreidian could see now that they meant well, but he was in a rather foul mood.

Then there was a roar. The people looked up. Mr. Kamenev was back with his noisy tractor, pulling a long wooden pallet. The villagers lifted the Lizardanian onto the pallet, dragging the great burden to the village church, the regional hospital being in their estimation much too far away. Worn out and rather amused by the efforts of the people, the Lizardanian did not resist. Once there at the church, he gathered himself, rose and allowed them to lead him inside. The people supported and guided him to the alter table, the only surface deemed large and strong enough to hold him. Soreidian rolled atop it and the old table creaked beneath his tremendous weight. But it did not break.

"He must weigh 700 pounds!" said they. The real number was nearly 800.

The little Russian girl who had first reported the battle now seemed to take a personal interest in Soreidian's wounds. Too weak to prevent it, he watched helplessly as the villagers experimented with different remedies for his injuries and the little girl dabbed at his forehead and the Crocodilian's claw slashes with a cold cloth.

"What is your name?" said Soreidian to the little girl-doctor in English.

The girl did not reply, but smiled down. She continued her work in great concentration.

Soreidian began to wonder if *Universalian* would work and so tried that.

But the little girl only smiled again. She seemed about six or seven years old. He scolded himself for failing to learn more about the people he had helped to save. Now they were doing their best to save him. He was very moved and haunted by his former prejudices against us—and his pledges that he would never help humans.

"Do you have no one that understands English?" said the Lizardanian with frustration in *Universalian*, addressing the others around him. Comprehension was not noticeable on the faces of the kindly villagers. Careful with his pronunciation, he asked the girl her name again in very slow *Universalian*.

The little girl smiled again and said, "My name is Dena, Mr. Star Dragon," in French, this time. Soreidian picked out the name, repeated it, and the girl nodded. *Progress*, he reassured himself.

"You're very kind to me. I have never been particularly nice...to your people...not really," Soreidian told the little girl. A crowd of adults, which now included some nervous looking officials, went scurrying around the church, whispering and consulting in low voices. He convinced himself that he was confessing his sins before the whole race through this little Russian girl.

Somewhere a phone was ringing.

Little Dena took to arranging the bandages, with the concerned look of the junior healer, hard at work on her craft. Older people seemed to believe that stopping the bleeding was the first priority and this was tired at great pains.

"Hereafter," said Soreidian with an apology in back of his words, "If the stars permit me a hereafter that you can understand, I will think better of your kind and promise to give something back to your race," he knew the girl could understand only the gist of his words, but he thought it important to say anyway. Again a fresh, cold wash cloth was applied to his forehead—it felt remarkably soothing, and the great sprawling "star dragon" lay on the alter, bewitched by the child Dena and her constant attendance to his hurts. Brian and I had won him over without even being there.

There were now two doctors in the room before the Lizardanian patient, but they only argued between themselves about the best course of treatment, leaving Dena and several elderly women to actually do the tending.

"Further, I will learn these human languages and come back to your village and express my thanks — and in meaningful ways too — I notice that you don't have here — I can *build* you — " but the little blond girl only put a finger to her lips. Soreidian obediently stopped talking. Dena beamed. The elderly women were equally taken by the roll of nursemaid played by the girl. Dena pressed the cold wash cloth closer to Soreidian's apparently wet eyes. He assured me there were no tears (right!).

Minutes later, there was commotion at the church entrance.

A team of Lizardanians and Alligatorians came into the little building with an escort of enthusiastic villagers.

"Soreidian," said Torrillian "you have your own nurse, you certainly don't need us!" they teased him seeing that while his wounds were very severe, they no longer threatened his life. Soreidian fidgeted in embarrassment — but he did not shy from Dena's insistent attention, even in front of the newcomers. Exhaustion took its full toll on pride.

XI

The villagers in the field looked down at the dead Crocodilian. Murmurs within the crowd carried the idea that it would go hard on the village if some of this kind of star dragon came looking for him. A large hole was quickly dug in the snowy field with the help of a backhoe from Kamenev's. The prodigious creature was rolled into the earth, this one being even heavier than the Lizardanian, it taken nearly everyone present to perform the task. The grave was hastily covered — but not marked.

CHAPTER FOURTEEN
Companionship

As the remaining Crocodilians fighters and cruisers turned away from the curious blue world of primitives, cries for joy echoed across the planet.

Tiperia landed in the ocean — aboard, I was amazed at the gentleness of this landing. Several smaller allied ships arrived before our impact to slow our decent. They lodged themselves under Tiperia's now extended wings, their thrusters easing the impact on the ocean. We went out on the surface of *Tiperia* and a sight I will never forget met my eyes. It seemed that every sea creature known was at the surface, or near it, expressing gratitude to *Tiperia*. There was nothing else to call it. The whales were what amazed us humans, and the sounds they made. The aliens didn't seem all that surprised. You could just tell.

The rock and metal that hit the Earth had done great damage and lives were lost, but the price was small compared with planet-death. Humanity used Lizardanian technology to neutralize the resultant radiation, many days being required for this task. It was a great hardship on millions, the waiting for the decontamination to take place. Many grieved as the world's airmen list was read. Due to the destruction of some of the Lizardanian laser towers by the Crocodilians, many other military service members from all nations also were lost. The Lizardanians were much aggrieved by their own deaths which came to almost 250 souls, an incredible number to a race of only a thousand and one for whom death was a very rare occurrence. The Seree, Orcharia and Parcharians had also lost vessels and many lives.

The unexpected suffering to both the Lizardanians and their friends cast a pale over the celebrations, but in general joy was great. Most of the two asteroids had been blown into less destructive pieces and generally scattered, well before impacting our saved Earth.

"I knew you'd turn up, despite what you think to the contrary! It's *jolly!*" said I to Katrina, affecting an English accent, as we meet at her Uncle's house back in Vermont. My small family and the Chakiayas were mingling with some of the aliens, getting some first hand experience with *Universalian.* Even my dad had shown up. Katrina had hugged her father and mother harder than ever with her famous bear hug, such that they had to beg for her tender mercies.

"Oh, sure, right—NOT!" Katrina said to me with her hearty laugh. "But I was actually afraid the entire time that the Parcharia wouldn't come back with me. Then they saw that I would be going back alone. So they decided that we really must be worth helping. Kind of crazy reasoning on their part."

"Hey, can 100 billion people be wrong?" Then I swallowed, knowing it was now or never. I couldn't let her escape again. "Do you feel the same about that date?"

"Well, you're sure your companion no longer requires company every second of the day?" asked she. "And what about Soreidian, how is he?"

"I think Soreidian is fine. And I think Littorian can be left on his own for a few hours…but," I added more gravely, "I think we'd better try to keep close to them now, you know. For instance, I understand there is talk of giving out medals and all kinds of crap like that…oh, and it's okay to say 'crap,' generally — it's not that bad a word."

"But for someone ready to give his life for other humans, do you have that low a view of our own kind? What do you think, that we'll get hold of them and corrupt them or something? You underestimate them. They know what we can be like, despite what we said and sang," she asked it sarcastically, tossing back her hair back.

"I'm just afraid we have a long way to go to prove that things Soreidian said aren't true. After all, Lizardanians and the Seree have taken back their technology and have stripped Earth's military of all the modifications they'd made. Now we have no dangerous nuclear weapons — but the Crocodilians now hate us. If they know we're defenseless now, what do you think they'll do to us, first chance they get? It seems like every time I try to make things better they get…well…better *and* worse. Don't you think we need Lizardania now more than ever?"

"But do they need us, Brian — really?"

"We'll prove it to them. I'm ready if you are. But what comes next?"

Katrina thought a moment and looked into the snowy woods in Uncle Vanya's long back yard.

"Easy," said she with a grin, adjusting the hood on her cloak to protect her rosy cheeks from the rising wind. The pine trees swayed nearby, creaking. "We'll learn who The Thirty are and then we'll explain to Lizardania why they should stay here. We need our own Thirty, Brian, it's not fair that we can't find some young people in tough circumstances, some thoughtful kids who feel like we do. Maybe…some on drugs, Brian. You know, that it's better to stay here and improve our world, rather than running off to the stars with the Lizardanians. Not that we can't visit them, I'd love to do that—but we can't abandon Earth."

"Yeah, but what do The Thirty want? We've never met them."

"I fear the future with them in it," said Katrina quietly.

"I know, me too—we just started a war, you know—won't they say that's all the more reason to go?"

"We ended a war, Brian Miller," Katrina looked at me solemnly. "We saved our world, just a couple of teenagers!"

"But what have we saved it *for*?" I asked.

"Life doesn't need a reason to want to continue," snapped Katrina, paraphrasing a Lizardanian saying that she'd recently learned. I felt her mind reach out to my troubled one.

"Don't shut me out," she whispered. The Lizardanians were looking out into it, toward Har'dack Hill, through Uncle Vanya's windows. Lizardanian food had been produced and the humans around the big front room were sampling it. It's just the *best* stuff you ever ate—truly!

"Sorry, I'm just worried. I guess I'm a worrier. So we should ask Littorian about expanding the Companion Program?"

"Companion Program?" Katrina looked at me with her curious glance, characterized by the side of her lip curling into something like a smile, something like a smirk.

"Yeah. Got a better name? Besides, it was you who said 'companion.'"

"Well, ah...I guess that will work. Maybe you better ask your buddy Justin for a better idea."

I laughed. "I don't think so."

"And we'll ask them to stay — say for a year?"

"I'd like that, but I don't think they will. The pull of the stars is too great for them. Think about *Tiperia*, I'm sure she, or it, or whatever, wants to move on. *Tiperia* really saved us, at the end, you know. And I want to see those stars, too — think of it! Lizardania knows so many worlds. Besides, do we want them to be exposed to, you know, all the awful things about this world. We've failed and are failing in many ways. And you and I — we didn't win a single one of our debates on the merits of the arguments, you know," I looked from the yard into the Chakiaya home. The aliens and the humans, I had to admit, were engaged in conversation in a most friendly fashion. But could that last? Should it? I even saw Principal Brodsky now in the great living room, and that made me smile. He had really helped me, when I was at my lowest low.

"Yes we did, we did win one of the sessions," corrected Katrina, giving me a playful shove.

"I said *on the merits*," was my serious reply, pushing back. "But I guess they were impressed by the way we fought for life."

"Life..." Katrina looked at her hands, once soaked with her own and Alligatorian blood. It seemed centuries ago.

227

"…is precious," I finished for her, since she seemed unlikely to finish herself.

"We need to see the Lizardanians and ask about what happens now." And then she shoved me playfully again, and this time I slipped (and only *slipped*, by the way!), falling in the snow.

I looked up at my friend. She reached down and pulled me up. We moved closer, our eyes perfectly aligned. She bent toward me, the eyes beginning to close. I could feel her warm breath—

"Brian and Katrina! I'm glad I found you…quickly now," it was Torrillian walking into the backyard. We jerked away from each other as though guilty of something. It took me a moment to snap out of it, so eager was I to kiss her.

None other than Leah Starblue and Joe Triassic followed into the snowy yard!

"This will be the last time you will see your teachers masquerading as humans…for they have taken companions," and at the words, Mr. Triassic and Ms. Starblue melted into Soreidian and Danillia.

"I'd like you to meet the leaders of The Thirty, the companions of Soreidian and Danillia," said Torrillian, a little gravely.

Katrina and I exchanged quick, guarded glanced and steeled ourselves. This we hadn't expected. And we swallowed in our dry throats and watched the corner of Uncle Vanya's house. Around this corner now came two youths. Their capes and the light cascading Lizardanian robes, streamed out behind them.

The two were clearly teenagers, but the exact age was a hard to judge. I still don't know, and I guess I should. They could have been thirteen or nineteen. Their faces were smooth, the boy's tanned, the girl very white against particularly rosy cheeks. The blond young man with very light blue eyes came up level with me. I had not encountered such a look of unabashed appraisal before, even against the Mack gang. I was being sized up, the real Brian Miller being compared with the televised version, now the darling of the media, a hero to the world, along with the marvelous Russian girl, Katrina. The young woman, walking even more quickly came face-to-face with Katrina. Her cobalt blue robes danced lightly above the fresh snow. She abruptly extended a hand — gloved in Lizardanian fabric, like Katrina's. "It is an honor to finally meet you, Katrina," said she softly, a tad too sweetly for the Russian, I could tell.

I was similarly confronted a moment later.

"Brian Miller. I've watched you and can only thank you, like all humans everywhere. You're given us a great chance."

'Us,' thought I to Katrina. *And 'can only thank you,'…why's that — because he can't get away with saying anything else?*

I don't know, this is very strange, she thought back to me. *Let's wait a bit and see…*

They're like the ice around us, was my reply.

"Brian, Katrina," said Torrillian eyeing us carefully, "this is Jason Shireman and Rachel Dreadnought."

Katrina and I exchanged another quick glance. With visible trepidation hands were outstretched. The Lizardanian custom which we practiced now was to raise a hand and lay it flat against another's. Then the fingers were clasped together with pressure of varying degree for the making of variety of impressions. We pairs of humans made this gesture now. Rachel was squeezing a bit too enthusiastically for Katrina's taste, but I knew the Russian was, too.

"Very good," said Torrillian, sounding rather relieved. "We'll meet with the rest of The Thirty to discuss the time of our departure," he said with finality. The two newcomers smiled at our shock. Now the snow, and our hearts, began to fall very heavily.

CHAPTER FIFTEEN
It Ought To Be Second Nature

The Lizardanians were gathered with The Thirty
at the Collins-Pearly Sports Arena on the edge of
Saint Albans City. The building stood just 15 miles
from the Canadian border. Another severe Vermont
winter storm was playing itself out. Even as a little
kid, I couldn't recall a colder winter. We had some
bad ones.

The interior of the arena held a hockey rink. A
group of young people stood near the center.
Representatives from the Alligatorians, Parcharia,
Seree and the Orcharia were also present, along with
the Lizardanians.

In walked Torrillian, with Katrina and I
following. We stopped at the rink's edge and caught
sight of The Thirty. They were dressed just like us.
Apparently, they had been waiting a long while.

The group of teens stared at Katrina and me.

These kids would have chosen to leave with
Lizardania, to turn their backs on Earth. Katrina and
I held that against them. We knew we could never be
friends.

Remember that we have been through the fire...and these damn kids haven't!

Katrina's reminder did not reassure me much.

While there was a mixture of races and cultures from all over the world among The Thirty, Katrina and I felt they all had something in common. The ratio of boys to girls was exactly equal.

They are the best, Katrina thought to me.

The best of the beast in us all, I thought back to her, eyeing them icily. *And didn't you just swear? What's up with that?*

I'm sorry. Again a bad habit I got from you. I'll master it yet!

Katrina shivered. I was staring at Jason. Jason returned my steady glare without expression. He didn't look like he'd ever been afraid of anything. Katrina wondered if something was being exchanged between us. Sure was — way.

Then Jason and Rachel slowly began hand movements. Katrina and I instinctively moved, too...to a place absent of weapons.

Torrillian noted the movement, and I regretted it.

But beginning with the very two we'd met in Uncle Vanya's backyard, a thunderous applause began. My staring at Jason broke. Katrina blushed and reaching out to me, took my hand. For all her courage, she was still shy. The Thirty came forward, smiling, reaching for us. The ovation was long, warm.

The applause slowly died and I looked to Katrina, with The Thirty all around us, expressing their appreciations and encouragements. They seemed only to want to touch Earth's saviors.

They want us...and I know I want to be with Littorian and Lizardania.

I know, thought the Russian. *I don't think we're done.*

I don't think we're done, either.

It's going to be hard…

Had I known it was going to be this hard, I would not have got into this.

Katrina looked from the crowd.

I think you would, Katrina thought to me.

I blinked, startled.

You can think to the hand! Besides, maybe I won't ask you out on that date!

Katrina looked down at the rink, then into my eyes.

I think you will…

The End